Samuel Johnson

THE HISTORY OF

Rasselas

PRINCE OF ABYSSINIA

edited, with an Introduction
by WARREN FLEISCHAUER

BARRON'S EDUCATIONAL SERIES, INC.

GREAT NECK, NEW YORK

Library of Congress Catalog Card No. 61-18208

22509

Contents

CONTENTS

CONTENTS

THE HISTORY OF

Rasselas

INTRODUCTION

"EVERY MAN," noted Hilaire Belloc (1925), "ought
to read *Rasselas*, and every wise man will read it
half a dozen times in his life. Indeed, a man would do
well to read it once a year at least, for never was wisdom
better put, or more enduringly." Even James Boswell,
with a narcissism hardly characteristic of a wise man,
had testified: "I am not satisfied if a year passes without
my having read it through; and at every perusal my
admiration of the mind which produced it is so highly
raised that I can scarcely believe that I had the honor
of enjoying the intimacy of such a man." Yet no one in
1791, when Boswell published his *Life of Johnson*, would
have been more astonished than the biographer to find
what is doubtless true — that his account of the writing
and publication of *Rasselas* is more familiar to today's
common reader than is that greatest of philosophic tales.

However, in commenting on *Rasselas*, Johnson's biog-
raphers, from the eighteenth century to the present,
have made too much of the mournfulness of the period
of its composition, and too little of the great heart,
born to endure, that could surmount its sorrows. Of
course, there can be no doubt that the death of Johnson's
mother, in January, 1759, at the age of ninety, though

long anticipated by him as "one of the few calamities on which I think with terror," as he had confided to Lucy Porter in 1749, was an experience made even more intensely excruciating by what he himself, in the inner reaches of his conscience, interpreted as filial neglect. There is every reason for us to accept the tradition transmitted by Boswell: "I have been told that he regretted much his not having gone to visit his mother for several years previous to her death." More precisely, Johnson had not seen her for twenty-two years, since 1737, when he had established himself permanently in London. But he had never forgotten her. Although the biographical record of this pre-Boswellian period is comparatively sparse, there is indication, as in Johnson's letter (May 6, 1755) to Bennet Langton, of his intentions: "I have a mother more than eighty years old, who has counted the days to the publication of my book [*The Dictionary*] in hopes of seeing me." And yet year melted imperceptibly into year; the twenty-six hour coach journey from London to Lichfield was never taken. Intermittent illness, hack drudgery, lexicographical toil, grinding poverty, and, possibly most of all, the inexplicable lassitude, which Johnson ever accounted his greatest curse, afflicted and immobilized him. True, with the publication of *The Dictionary*, Johnson had been irrevocably swept over the threshold of fame by 1755, but a year later Samuel Richardson had to rescue him from the fate of the debtors' prison. In 1759 Johnson had not the money, as William Strahan later informed Boswell, to "defray the expense of his mother's funeral and pay some little debts which she had left."

So it is that, in R. W. Chapman's edition of Johnson's *Letters*, even more than in the biographies, we are struck

by the businesslike tone of the note, incongruously
thrust amid epistles of pious grief and dated January 20,
1759, offering Strahan for publication "a thing which I
was preparing for the press," to be titled "The Choice
of Life or the History of ——— Prince of Abissinia."
Of the composition of this little book, we can know
only what the author told Sir Joshua Reynolds, "that
he composed it in the evenings of one week" and "sent
it to the press in portions as it was written." Whatever
the reason for the delay, *Rasselas* was not published
until April 19, though in time to be praised by *The
Gentleman's Magazine* for that month as presenting ' the
most elegant and striking pictures of life and nature, the
most acute disquisitions, and the happiest illustrations
of the most important truths."

Now the above sparse and contradictory history of
Rasselas is valuable, not to show that the tale was, as
Sir John Hawkins suggested, the sublimation of Johnson's personal grief for the death of his mother, but only
rather to supply us with information about the occasion
of the composition of the book which Samuel Johson
had been writing, with his heart-beats, all of his life.
We need not peer with Hawkins into the "time . . .
when the heavy hand of affliction bore him down" to
account for the philosophy and tone which pervade
Rasselas. We can more profitably pore, as Joseph Wood
Krutch advises, on "Johnson's recorded sayings" from
which "another *Rasselas* could easily be complied," or,
as James L. Clifford asserts, on *The Vanity of Human
Wishes*, in which, ten years earlier (1749), Johnson had
eloquently set forth its basic theme. Even more amply,
in the essays of *The Rambler*, *The Adventurer*, and *The
Idler*, the modern reader can trace the resources of re-

flection upon which Johnson's novel draws. In short, *Rasselas* is not the articulation of a temporary mood of despondent grief. Nor is it even, as Boswell implies with the delicacy of a double negative, the reflection of a permanent psychological infirmity: "Notwithstanding my high admiration of *Rasselas*, I will not maintain that the 'morbid melancholy' in Johnson's constitution may not, perhaps, have made life appear to him more insipid and unhappy than it generally is." Johnson's vision of life was, in fact, more penetrating, more courageous, and more deeply rooted in the wisdom of the species than either Hawkins or Boswell imagined. We do not attribute to grief at his mother's death the cry of the preacher who is Ecclesiastes, that all is vanity and vexation of spirit, nor to constitutional melancholy the turbid ebb and flow of human misery that Sophocles heard long ago on the Aegean.

Yet if we must have a literary source for *Rasselas*, then we may turn not, as has become superficially customary, to Johnson's 1734 translation of the French abridgment of the Portuguese Jesuit Father Lobo's *Voyage to Abyssinia*, but rather to the book by the nonjuring divine who so profoundly stirred Johnson as an Oxford undergraduate. William Law's *Serious Call to a Holy Life* (1728), according to Johnson's own testimony, set him to "thinking in earnest of religion" for the first time "after I became capable of rational inquiry." Of Law, who had a memorable effect also on John Wesley and George Whitefield, Edward Gibbon later observed: "If he finds a spark of piety in his reader's mind, he will soon kindle it to a flame." So it was from the *Serious Call* (Chapter 13) that Johnson learned, as Law had urged, to profit "by the follies of the world" and to learn "the greatness of Religion, from the littleness and vanity of every other way of life." Thirty years later these lessons became the foundations of *Rasselas*.

It is indeed easier, though not so essential, to demonstrate other literary influences upon *Rasselas*, to place it, for example, in the genre of the Eastern tale (e.g., Voltaire's *Zadig*), which had much vogue throughout the period and which Johnson himself had previously written (*The Rambler*, Nos. 65, 120, 190, 204, 205; *The Idler*, Nos. 75, 99, 101). Further, *Rasselas* has been related to satire of the type of the *ingenu* hero (cf. Swift's *Gulliver's Travels*), and it is doubtless that rarest kind of fiction, the unabashedly philosophical novel (cf. Santayana's *The Last Puritan*). Most often, of course, it has been coupled with Voltaire's *Candide* (1759), to which, despite a certain specious resemblance, it owes nothing. The heart and pulse of *Rasselas* are rather to be found in Law's question, propounded in print long before, to the "mad and violent," the "miserably poor" student of Pembroke College, Oxford: "What greater motive to a religious life than the vanity, the poorness of all worldly enjoyments?"

It is the delusion of "all wordly enjoyments" that *Rasselas* conclusively strips bare, and it is significant that its opening scene is an Ethiopian Happy Valley. Johnson probably recurs to a tradition finding expression in *Paradise Lost* (IV, 280-284). There Milton denies that the Garden of Eden can be geographically located

> . . . *where Abassin kings their issue guard,*
> *Mount Amara, though this by some supposed*

True Paradise, under the Ethiop line
By Nilus' head, enclosed with shining rock,
A whole day's journey high . . .

Like Milton's Amara, Johnson's valley, where "every
desire was immediately granted," is not Eden, nor is it
El Dorado, the rationalistic Utopia, which Voltaire's
Candide reaches in mid-narrative. Johnson was too ortho-
dox a Christian to conceive even of a fictional happy
valley. "Infelicity is involved in corporeal nature, and
interwoven with our being," Johnson had observed in
The Rambler, No. 32; and Boswell, in one of his more
critically perceptive moments, remarks accurately: "To
those who . . . maintain that human nature has not
fallen from the state in which it was created, the instruction of this sublime story will be of no avail."
However it may be pleasant, the Happy Valley is inhabited by beings all too human who, as a species, are
alienated from the source of happiness. So (Chapter 12)
Imlac informs his prince that he knows "not one of all
your attendants who does not lament the hour when he
entered this retreat," and Nekayah begs (Chapter 14)
to flee "this tasteless tranquillity." The Happy Valley
is not Eden, which is nowhere to be found. This home
truth is made evident to Rasselas even before he and his
party have fled the valley, for they have the assurance
of honest Imlac (Chapter 11) that "human life is everywhere a state in which much is to be endured, and little
to be enjoyed." From all of Johnson's works no observation has been quoted more often to indicate his constitutional melancholy; but, as Johnson himself had
earlier (*The Adventurer*, No. 120) remarked: "There is . . .
no topic on which it is more superfluous to accumulate

authorities, nor any assertion of which our own eyes will more easily discover or our sensations more frequently impress the truth, than that misery is the lot of man, that our present state is a state of danger and infelicity."

In his making such statements, Johnson was well aware that he was out of tune with much of the influential thought of his own time. "The fiction of happiness is propagated by every tongue," he had observed in *The Idler* (No. 18); and the "reflections," "epistles," "systems," "essays," "arts," and "discourses," written on and of happiness, as listed by Paul Hazard (*European Thought in the Eighteenth Century*, Chapter ii), indicate the extent of Johnson's reaction to contemporary intellectual currents sweeping toward triumph in the French Revolution. "Hell is no more," exulted Helvetius' Oromaze; " 'tis Heaven now on earth!" Happiness, the youthful revolutionary St. Just was to explain solemnly to the Convention, was "*un idée neuve en Europe*" — a new idea in Europe. To Johnson, happiness was not new, but an ageless yearning in the hearts of Adam's progeny; it was not an idea, but a delusion. So in *Rasselas* he wrote a parable for his century.

In quest of happiness, Rasselas and his party set forth from the Happy Valley. The plot is simple, that of a picaresque novel in miniature, though without a rogue as hero, ranging through all the basic conditions and ethical conceptions of life. But the plot is slow to generate, because Johnson must compound ennui from satiety, desire from ennui, action from desire, experience from action, wisdom from experience. Between a fourth and a third of the tale is consumed by its motivation, but Johnson artfully avoids boredom by achieving variety through the dissertation on flying (Chapter 6) and through the history of Imlac (Chapters 9 through 13). This latter digression, actually no digression but the microcosm of the tale about to unfold, is itself interrupted by the noble dissertation on poetry (Chapter 10). Yet such is Johnson's art that, though we are diverted, we are never led astray. While Johnson is qualifying Imlac as a sage mentor, he is also establishing the prince as an eager inquirer; while he is revealing Imlac's wisdom, its basis and extent, he is quickening Rasselas' desire.

In majestic time, the prince and his retinue arrive at Cairo (Chapter 16). From this point *Rasselas* becomes, according to G. K. Chesterton, "an ironic tale of the disillusionments of a youth among the pompous dignities and philosophies of this world." A gross hedonism (Chapter 17) is too base for the noble prince, who, at the same time (Chapter 18), is too honestly human for a stoicism fraudulently Olympian. The beam of Diogenes' lantern is directed into that Cynic's tub (Chapter 21), which is found hollow, and (Chapter 22) the life according to nature (Bolingbroke, Rousseau, *et al*) proves to be ridiculously incoherent, baffling, and incomprehensible. From philosophies at variance with life, the prince directs his inquiry toward life itself. Turning his back on the metropolis, he fruitlessly tours the countryside. The pastoral life of simplicity and tranquillity, the Arcadia of the poets, is (Chapter 19) clouded with boorishness and ignorance, cankered with envy and discontent; but the court of the Bassa (Chapter 24) is racked by a malignancy distinguished only by its refined subtlety. Prosperity (Chapter 20) is devoured by power, and power (Chapter 24) is, in turn, destroyed by the greater power

of the Sultan, who himself is assassinated. The humble
joys of domestic life (Chapters 25 and 26) are as delusory
as those of high station (Chapter 27). In human attach-
ments, which must be sought if one is not to endure the
wretchedness of solitude (Chapter 21) and of madness
(Chapter 44), there are inevitable, in the course of sad
time, miseries no less certain (Chapter 36) than those
which age (Chapter 45), coming unbidden, thrusts upon
man. Johnson's canvass of stations and philosophies of
life is exhaustive.

At this point the reader may return, hopefully, to
Imlac's assertion that "human life is everywhere a state
in which much is to be endured, and little to be enjoyed." After all, there is something, however little, to
be enjoyed. But even this consolation is checked by
Nekayah's question (Chapter 36): "Yet what is to be
expected from our pursuit of happiness, when we find
the state of life to be such that happiness itself is the
cause of misery?" However, Imlac, in his wisdom, had
already anticipated the answer to this question (Chapter
16): "We are long before we are convinced that happiness
is never to be found." In truth, we are long. We are
longer than was Nekayah, far longer than is our vicari-
ous experience through Nekayah; we are longer, as
Johnson himself perhaps realized, than the forty-nine
chapters of *Rasselas*, than the forty-nine years he was of
age when he penned the conclusion in which nothing
is concluded.

Because hope does indeed spring eternally in the human breast, Johnson wisely does not bring his plot to a
full stop. In the final chapter, Rasselas desires "a little
kingdom, in which he might administer justice in his
own person, and see all the parts of government with

his own eyes." However, adds Johnson, with sad humor and soft understatement, "he could never fix the limits of his dominion, and was always adding to the number of his subjects." The prince has had this delusion before (Chapter 8); has since seen exposed the vanity of greatness (Chapter 27); has, in renouncing it, confessed the horrifying extent to which it has corrupted him (Chapter 44); and yet (Chapter 49) has permitted it to return only to concede, in the final paragraph of the tale, that it is a wish which cannot be obtained. But perhaps it really does not matter, for the unwritten irony is the probability that the prince is called to the station, not which he chooses, but to which he was born and which he must, as best he can, endure with the assistance of a philosophy other than those which he has rejected.

The Johnsonian solution has been labeled by one critic as "Christian stoicism," and this phrase, in its loose use of the word 'stoicism," is near the mark, though it would not be acceptable to so discriminating a master of words as Johnson, whose great *Dictionary* defines "Stoick" only as "a philosopher who followed the sect of Zeno; holding the neutrality of external things." Against such stoicism, no one in the whole of the eighteenth century lashed out more fiercely than did the author of *Rasselas* (Chapter 18). In *The Rambler* (No. 6) Johnson had earlier noted "that man should never suffer his happiness to depend upon external circumstances is one of the chief precepts of the Stoical philosophy; . . . it is overthrown by the experience of every hour, and the powers of nature rise up against it;" and again (No. 47), when he had asserted that "an attempt to preserve life in a state of neutrality and indifference is unreasonable and vain." A word better than "stoicism," as George Saintsbury once suggested, is "resignation," but the Johnsonian word is "patience," though one must "remember," as Nekayah warned (Chapter 27), "that patience must suppose pain."

Even so, as David Nichol Smith recently informed the Johnson Society of Lichfield, in a Presidential address, "I have never heard of anyone competent to understand [*Rasselas*] who found it depressing." Among its eighteenth-century readers, there were those who were "competent," like Sir Joshua Reynolds, who enthusiastically proclaimed that the tale was "writ by an angel," just as there were those who, like Mrs. Chapone, were sure that it would "extinguish hope, and consequently industry." But there were also those who, like Boswell, could deprecate Johnson's tragic view of life as "more insipid and unhappy than it generally is," and who yet at the same time could see that "Johnson meant, by showing the unsatisfactory nature of things temporal, to direct the hopes of man to things eternal."

Every reader of *Rasselas* must note and mark well that its penultimate scene is set, scarcely by accident, in the catacombs of Cairo, to which the prince's party has descended that Imlac might discourse on the nature of the soul: "That it will not perish by any inherent cause of decay, or principle of corruption, may be known by philosophy; but philosophy can tell no more." There is, Imlac adds, a "higher authority," meaning divine revelation, and here, on the bourne of eternity, the quest for happiness is brought to a stand, though life itself must go on, struggling, as the prince and his party struggle, up the life-giving waters of the Nile, against the current, to return to the Happy Valley that is not really happy. As the person "competent" to read *Ras-*

selas perceives the paradox of even the wise Imlac braving the tide of the Nile, while he is "driven along the stream of life," he experiences, without the grand trappings of tragedy, something akin to tragic purgation, a chastening of the spirit. The illusions of youth, if not obliterated, have been at least tempered and moderated; the wisdom of age and of the ages confirmed.

Warren Fleischauer

C. W. Post College
Long Island University
Brookville, New York
February 17, 1961

Description of a Palace in a Valley

I YE who listen with credulity to the whispers of fancy and pursue with eagerness the phantoms of hope, who expect that age will perform the promises of youth and that the deficiencies of the present day will be supplied by the morrow, — attend to the history of Rasselas, prince of Abyssinia.

Rasselas was the fourth son of the mighty emperor, in whose dominions the Father of Waters begins his course; whose bounty pours down the streams of plenty and scatters over half the world the harvests of Egypt.

According to the custom which has descended from age to age among the monarchs of the torrid zone, Rasselas was confined in a private palace with the other sons and daughters of Abyssinian royalty, till the order of succession should call him to the throne.

The place which the wisdom or policy of antiquity had destined for the residence of the Abyssinian princes was a spacious valley in the kingdom of Amhara, surrounded on every side by mountains, of which the summits overhang the middle part. The only passage by which it could be entered was a cavern that passed under a rock, of which it has long been disputed whether it was the work of nature or of human industry. The outlet of the cavern was concealed by a thick wood, and the mouth which opened into the valley was closed with gates of iron, forged by the artificers of ancient days, so massy that no man could without the help of engines open or shut them.

From the mountains on every side, rivulets descendedthat filled all the valley with verdure and fertility, and formed a lake in the middle, inhabited by fish of every species and frequented by every fowl whom nature has taught to dip the wing in water. This lake discharged its superfluities by a stream which entered a dark cleft of the mountain on the northern side and fell with dreadful noise from precipice to precipice, till it was heard no more.

The sides of the mountains were covered with trees; the banks of the brooks were diversified with flowers; every blast shook spices from the rocks, and every month dropped fruits upon the ground. All animals that bite the grass or browse the shrub, whether wild or tame, wandered in this extensive circuit, secured from beasts of prey by the mountains which confined them. On one part were flocks and herds feeding in the pastures, on another all the beasts of chase frisking in the lawns; the sprightly kid was bounding on the rocks, the subtle monkey frolicking in the trees, and the solemn elephant reposing in the shade. All the diversities of the world were brought together; the blessings of nature were collected, and its evils extracted and excluded.

The valley, wide and fruitful, supplied its inhabitants with the necessaries of life, and all delights and superfluities were added at the annual visit which the emperor paid his children, when the iron gate was opened to the sound of music; and, during eight days, everyone that resided in the valley was required to propose whatever might contribute to make seclusion pleasant, to fill up the vacancies of attention and lessen the tediousness of time. Every desire was immediately granted. All the artificers of pleasure were called to gladden the festivity; the musicians exerted the power of harmony, and the dancers showed their activity before the princes, in hope that they should pass their lives in this blissful captivity, to which those only were admitted whose performance was thought able to add novelty to luxury. Such was the appearance of security and delight which this retirement afforded that they to whom it was new always desired that it might be perpetual; and, as those on whom the iron gate had once closed were never suffered to return, the effect of longer experience could not be known. Thus every year produced new schemes of delight and new competitors for imprisonment.

The palace stood on an eminence raised about thirty paces above the surface of the lake. It was divided into many squares or courts, built with greater or less magnificence according to the rank of those for whom they were designed. The roofs were turned into arches of massy stone, joined by a cement that grew harder by time, and the building stood from century to century, deriding the solstitial rains and equinoctial hurricanes, without need of reparation.

This house, which was so large as to be fully known to none but some ancient officers who successively inherited the secrets of the place, was built as if suspicion herself had dictated the plan. To every room there was an open and secret passage; every square had a communication with the rest, either from the upper stories by private galleries or by subterranean passages from the lower apartments. Many of the columns had unsuspected cavities, in which a long race of monarchs had deposited their treasures. They then closed up the opening with marble, which was never to be removed but in the utmost exigencies of the kingdom, and recorded their accumulations in a book, which was itself concealed in a tower, not entered but by the emperor attended by the prince who stood next in succession.

The Discontent of Rasselas
in the Happy Valley

2 HERE the sons and daughters of Abyssinia lived only to know the soft vicissitudes of pleasure and repose, attended by all that were skilful to delight, and gratified with whatever the senses can enjoy. They wandered in gardens of fragrance and slept in the fortresses of security. Every art was practiced to make them pleased with their own condition. The sages who instructed them told them of nothing but the miseries of public life, and described all beyond the mountains as regions of calamity, where discord was always raging and where man preyed upon man.

To heighten their opinion of their own felicity, they were daily entertained with songs, the subject of which was *the happy valley*. Their appetites were excited by frequent enumerations of different enjoyments, and revelry and merriment was the business of every hour, from the dawn of morning to the close of even.

These methods were generally successful: few of the princes had ever wished to enlarge their bounds, but passed their lives in full conviction that they had all within their reach that art or nature could bestow, and pitied those whom fate had excluded from this seat of tranquillity as the sport of chance and the slaves of misery.

Thus they rose in the morning and lay down at night, pleased with each other and with themselves, — all but Rasselas, who, in the twenty-sixth year of his age, began to withdraw himself from their pastimes and assemblies, and to delight in solitary walks and silent meditation. He often sat before tables covered with luxury, and forgot to taste the dainties that were placed before him; he rose abruptly in the midst of the song, and hastily retired beyond the sound of music. His attendants observed the change and endeavored to renew his love of pleasure; he neglected their officiousness, repulsed their invitations, and spent day after day on the banks of rivulets sheltered with trees, where he sometimes listened to the birds in the branches, sometimes observed the fish playing in the stream, and anon cast his eyes upon the pastures and mountains filled with animals, of which some were biting the herbage and some sleeping among the bushes.

This singularity of his humor made him much observed. One of the sages, in whose conversation he had formerly delighted, followed him secretly in hope of discovering the cause of his disquiet. Rasselas, who knew not that anyone was near him, having for some time fixed his eyes upon the goats that were browsing among the rocks, began to compare their condition with his own.

"What," said he, "makes the difference between man and all the rest of the animal creation? Every beast that strays beside me has the same corporeal necessities with myself: he is hungry and crops the grass; he is thirsty and drinks the stream; his thirst and hunger are appeased; he is satisfied and sleeps; he arises again and is hungry; he is again fed and is at rest. I am hungry and thirsty like him, but when thirst and hunger cease, I am not at rest; I am like him pained with want, but am not like him satisfied with fullness. The intermediate hours are tedious and gloomy; I long again to be hungry that I may again quicken my attention. The birds peck the berries or the corn, and fly away to the groves, where they sit in seeming happiness on the branches and waste their lives in tuning one unvaried series of sounds. I likewise can call the lutanist and the singer; but the sounds that pleased me yesterday weary me today, and will grow yet more wearisome tomorrow. I can discover within me no power of perception which is not glutted with its proper pleasure; yet I do not feel myself delighted. Man surely has some latent sense for which this place affords no gratification, or he has some desires distinct from sense, which must be satisfied before he can be happy."

After this he lifted up his head and, seeing the moon rising, walked towards the palace. As he passed through the fields and saw the animals around him, "Ye," said he, "are happy, and need not envy me that walk thus among you, burdened with myself; nor do I, ye gentle beings, envy your felicity, for it is not the felicity of man. I have many distresses from which ye are free; I fear pain when I do not feel it; I sometimes shrink at evils recollected and sometimes start at evils anticipated. Surely the equity of Providence has balanced peculiar sufferings with peculiar enjoyments.''

With observations like these the prince amused himself as he returned, uttering them with a plaintive voice, yet with a look that discovered him to feel some complacence in his own perspicacity and to receive some solace of the miseries of life from consciousness of the delicacy with which he felt and the eloquence with which he bewailed them. He mingled cheerfully in the diversions of the evening, and all rejoiced to find that his heart was lightened.

The Wants of Him That Wants Nothing

3 ON the next day, his old instructor, imagining that he had now made himself acquainted with his disease of mind, was in hope of curing it by counsel, and officiously sought an opportunity of conference, which the prince, having long considered him as one whose intellects were exhausted, was not very willing to afford. "Why," said he, "does this man thus intrude upon me? Shall I be never suffered to forget those lectures which pleased only while they were new and, to become new again, must be forgotten?" He then walked into the wood and composed himself to his usual meditations, when, before his thoughts had taken any settled form, he perceived his pursuer at his side, and was at first prompted by his impatience to go hastily away; but, being unwilling to offend a man whom he had once reverenced and still loved, he invited him to sit down with him on the bank.

The old man, thus encouraged, began to lament the change which had been lately observed in the prince, and to inquire why he so often retired from the pleasures of the palace to loneliness and silence. "I fly from pleasure," said the prince, "because pleasure has ceased to please; I am lonely, because I am miserable and am unwilling to cloud with my presence the happiness of others." "You, sir," said the sage, "are the first who has complained of misery in the *happy valley*. I hope to convince you that your complaints have no real cause. You are here in full possession of all that the emperor of Abyssinia can bestow; here is neither labor to be endured, nor danger to be dreaded, yet here is all that labor or danger can procure or purchase. Look round, and tell me which of your wants is without supply. If you want nothing, how are you unhappy?"

"That I want nothing," said the prince, "or that I know not what I want, is the cause of my complaint. If I had any known want, I should have a certain wish; that wish would excite endeavor, and I should not then repine to see the sun move so slowly towards the western mountain, or lament when the day breaks and sleep will no longer hide me from myself. When I see the kids and the lambs chasing one another, I fancy that I should be happy if I had something to pursue. But, possessing all that I can want, I find one day and one hour exactly like another, except that the latter is still more tedious than the former. Let your experience inform me how the day may now seem as short as in my childhood, while nature was yet fresh and every moment showed me what I never had observed before. I have already enjoyed too much; give me something to desire."

The old man was surprised at this new species of affliction, and knew not what to reply, yet was unwilling to be silent. "Sir," said he, "if you had seen the miseries of the world, you would know how to value your present state." "Now," said the prince, "you have given me something to desire; I shall long to see the miseries of the world, since the sight of them is necessary to happiness."

The Prince Continues to Grieve and Muse

4 AT this time the sound of music proclaimed the hour of repast, and the conversation was concluded. The old man went away sufficiently discontented, to find that his reasonings had produced the only conclusion which they were intended to prevent. But in the decline of life shame and grief are of short duration, whether it be that we bear easily what we have borne long; or that, finding ourselves in age less regarded, we less regard others; or that we look with slight regard upon afflictions to which we know that the hand of death is about to put an end.

The prince, whose views were extended to a wider space, could not speedily quiet his emotions. He had been before terrified at the length of life which nature promised him, because he considered that in a long time much must be endured; he now rejoiced in his youth, because in many years much might be done.

The first beam of hope, that had been ever darted into his mind, rekindled youth in his cheeks and doubled the lustre of his eyes. He was fired with the desire of doing something, though he knew not yet with distinctness either end or means.

He was now no longer gloomy and unsocial; but, considering himself as master of a secret stock of happiness, which he could enjoy only by concealing it, he affected to be busy in all schemes of diversion, and endeavored to make others pleased with the state of which he himself was weary. But pleasures never can be so multiplied or continued as not to leave much of life unemployed; there were many hours, both of the night and day, which he could spend without suspicion in solitary thought. The load of life was much lightened; he went eagerly into the assemblies, because he supposed the frequency of his presence necessary to the success of his purposes; he retired gladly to privacy, because he had now a subject of thought.

His chief amusement was to picture to himself that world which he had never seen; to place himself in various conditions, to be entangled in imaginary difficulties, and to be engaged in wild adventures; but his benevolence always terminated his projects in the relief of distress, the detection of fraud, the defeat of oppression, and the diffusion of happiness.

Thus passed twenty months of the life of Rasselas. He busied himself so intensely in visionary bustle that he forgot his real solitude, and, amidst hourly preparations for the various incidents of human affairs, neglected to consider by what means he should mingle with mankind.

One day, as he was sitting on a bank, he feigned to himself an orphan virgin robbed of her little portion by a treacherous lover and crying after him for restitution and redress. So strongly was the image impressed upon his mind that he started up in the maid's defense, and ran forward to seize the plunderer, with all the eagerness of real pursuit. Fear naturally quickens the flight of guilt. Rasselas could not catch the fugitive with his utmost efforts; but, resolving to weary by perseverance him whom he could not surpass in speed, he pressed on till the foot of the mountain stopped his course.

Here he recollected himself and smiled at his own useless impetuosity. Then raising his eyes to the mountain, "This," said he, "is the fatal obstacle that hinders at once the enjoyment of pleasure and the exercise of virtue. How long is it that my hopes and wishes have flown beyond this boundary of my life, which yet I never have attempted to surmount!"

Struck with this reflection, he sat down to muse; and remembered that, since he first resolved to escape from his confinement, the sun had passed twice over him in his annual course. He now felt a degree of regret with which he had never been before acquainted. He considered how much might have been done in the time which had passed and left nothing real behind it. He compared twenty months with the life of man. "In life," said he, "is not to be counted the ignorance of infancy or

imbecility of age. We are long before we are able
to think, and we soon cease from the power of
acting. The true period of human existence may be
reasonably estimated at forty years, of which I
have mused away the four and twentieth part.
What I have lost was certain, for I have certainly
possessed it; but of twenty months to come, who
can assure me?"

The consciousness of his own folly pierced him
deeply, and he was long before he could be reconciled to himself. "The rest of my time," said he,
"has been lost by the crime or folly of my ancestors
and the absurd institutions of my country; I remember it with disgust, yet without remorse; but
the months that have passed since new light darted
into my soul, since I formed a scheme of reasonable
felicity, have been squandered by my own fault. I
have lost that which can never be restored; I have
seen the sun rise and set for twenty months, an
idle gazer on the light of heaven. In this time the
birds have left the nest of their mother and committed themselves to the woods and to the skies;
the kid has forsaken the teat and learned by degrees
to climb the rocks in quest of independent suste-
nance. I only have made no advances, but am still
helpless and ignorant. The moon, by more than
twenty changes, admonished me of the flux of life;
the stream that rolled before my feet upbraided my
inactivity. I sat feasting on intellectual luxury,
regardless alike of the examples of the earth and
the instructions of the planets. Twenty months are
passed. Who shall restore them?"

These sorrowful meditations fastened upon his

mind; he passed four months in resolving to lose no more time in idle resolves, and was awakened to more vigorous exertion by hearing a maid, who had broken a porcelain cup, remark that what cannot be repaired is not to be regretted.

This was obvious, and Rasselas reproached himself that he had not discovered it, having not known, or not considered how many useful hints are obtained by chance and how often the mind, hurried by her own ardor to distant views, neglects the truths that lie open before her. He for a few hours regretted his regret, and from that time bent his whole mind upon the means of escaping from the valley of happiness.

The Prince Meditates His Escape

5   HE now found that it would be very difficult to effect that which it was very easy to suppose effected. When he looked round about him, he saw himself confined by the bars of nature, which had never yet been broken, and by the gate, through which none that once had passed it were ever able to return. He was now impatient as an eagle in a grate. He passed week after week in clambering the mountains to see if there was any aperture which the bushes might conceal, but found all the summits inaccessible by their prominence. The iron gate he despaired to open, for it was not only secured with all the power of art, but was always watched by successive sentinels, and was by its position exposed to the perpetual observation of all the inhabitants.

He then examined the cavern through which the waters of the lake were discharged, and, looking down at a time when the sun shone strongly upon its mouth, he discovered it to be full of broken rocks which, though they permitted the stream to flow through many narrow passages, would stop any body of solid bulk. He returned discouraged and dejected, but, having now known the blessing of hope, resolved never to despair.

In these fruitless researches he spent ten months. The time, however, passed cheerfully away; in the morning he rose with new hope, in the evening applauded his own diligence, and in the night slept sound after his fatigue. He met a thousand amusements which beguiled his labor and diversified his thoughts. He discerned the various instincts of animals and properties of plants, and found the place replete with wonders of which he purposed to solace himself with the contemplation, if he should never be able to accomplish his flight; rejoicing that his endeavors, though yet unsuccessful, had supplied him with a source of inexhaustible inquiry.

But his original curiosity was not yet abated; he resolved to obtain some knowledge of the ways of men. His wish still continued, but his hope grew less. He ceased to survey any longer the walls of his prison, and spared to search by new toils for interstices which he knew could not be found, yet determined to keep his design always in view and lay hold on any expedient that time should offer.

A Dissertation on the Art of Flying

6   AMONG the artists that had been allured into the happy valley to labor for the accommodation and pleasure of its inhabitants, was a man eminent for his knowledge of the mechanic powers, who had contrived many engines both of use and recreation. By a wheel which the stream turned, he forced the water into a tower, whence it was distributed to all the apartments of the palace. He erected a pavilion in the garden, around which he kept the air always cool by artificial showers. One of the groves, appropriated to the ladies, was ventilated by fans, to which the rivulets that ran through it gave a constant motion; and instruments of soft music were placed at proper distances, of which some played by the impulse of the wind and some by the power of the stream.

This artist was sometimes visited by Rasselas, who was pleased with every kind of knowledge, imagining that the time would come when all his acquisitions should be of use to him in the open world. He came one day to amuse himself in his usual manner and found the master busy in building a sailing chariot; he saw that the design was practicable upon a level surface and, with expressions of great esteem, solicited its completion. The workman was pleased to find himself so much regarded by the prince and resolved to gain yet higher honors. "Sir," said he, "you have seen but a small part of what the mechanic sciences can perform. I have been long of opinion that, instead of the tardy conveyance of ships and chariots, man might use the swifter migration of wings; that the fields of air are open to knowledge and that only ignorance and idleness need crawl upon the ground."

This hint rekindled the prince's desire of passing the mountains. Having seen what the mechanist had already performed, he was willing to fancy that he could do more, yet resolved to inquire further before he suffered hope to afflict him by disappointment. "I am afraid," said he to the artist, "that your imagination prevails over your skill and that you now tell me rather what you wish than what you know. Every animal has his element assigned him; the birds have the air, and man and beasts the earth." "So," replied the mechanist, "fishes have the water, in which yet beasts can swim by nature and men by art. He that can swim needs not despair to fly; to swim is to fly in a grosser fluid, and to fly is to swim in a subtler. We are only to proportion our power of resistance to the different density of matter through which we are to pass. You will be necessarily upborne by the air, if you can renew any impulse upon it faster than the air can recede from the pressure."

"But the exercise of swimming," said the prince, "is very laborious; the strongest limbs are soon wearied. I am afraid the act of flying will be yet more violent, and wings will be of no great use unless we can fly further than we can swim."

"The labor of rising from the ground," said the artist, "will be great, as we see it in the heavier domestic fowls; but, as we mount higher, the earth's attraction and the body's gravity will be gradually diminished, till we shall arrive at a region where the man will float in the air without any tendency to fall. No care will then be necessary but to move forwards, which the gentlest impulse will effect. You, sir, whose curiosity is so extensive, will easily conceive with what pleasure a philosopher, furnished with wings and hovering in the sky, would see the earth and all its inhabitants rolling beneath him and presenting to him successively, by its diurnal motion, all the countries within the same parallel. How must it muse the pendent spectator to see the moving scene of land and ocean, cities and deserts! To survey with equal security the marts of trade and the fields of battle, mountains infested by barbarians, and fruitful regions gladdened by plenty and lulled by peace! How easily shall we then trace the Nile through all his passage, pass over to distant regions, and examine the face of nature from one extremity of the earth to the other!"

"All this," said the prince, "is much to be desired; but I am afraid that no man will be able to breathe in these regions of speculation and tranquillity. I have been told that respiration is difficult upon lofty mountains, yet from these precipices, though so high as to produce great tenuity of air, it is very easy to fall; therefore I suspect that, from any height where life can be supported, there may be danger of too quick descent."

"Nothing," replied the artist, "will ever be attempted, if all possible objections must be first overcome. If you will favor my project, I will try the first flight at my own hazard. I have considered the structure of all volant animals, and find the folding continuity of the bat's wings most easily accommodated to the human form. Upon this model I shall begin my task tomorrow and in a year expect to tower into the air beyond the malice and pursuit of man. But I will work only on this condition: that the art shall not be divulged and that you shall not require me to make wings for any but ourselves."

"Why," said Rasselas, "should you envy others so great an advantage? All skill ought to be exerted for universal good; every man has owed much to others, and ought to repay the kindness that he has received."

"If men were all virtuous," returned the artist, "I should with great alacrity teach them all to fly. But what would be the security of the good, if the bad could at pleasure invade them from the sky? Against an army sailing through the clouds, neither walls, nor mountains, nor seas could afford any security. A flight of northern savages might hover in the wind, and light at once with irresistible violence upon the capital of a fruitful region that was rolling under them. Even this valley, the retreat of princes, the abode of happiness, might be violated by the sudden descent of the naked nations that swarm on the coast of the southern sea.''

The prince promised secrecy, and waited for the performance, not wholly hopeless of success. He visited the work from time to time, observed its progress, and remarked many ingenious contrivances to facilitate motion and unite levity with strength. The artist was every day more certain that he should leave vultures and eagles behind him, and the contagion of his confidence seized upon the prince.

In a year the wings were finished; and, on a morning appointed, the maker appeared furnished for flight on a little promontory. He waved his pinions a while to gather air, then leaped from his stand, and in an instant dropped into the lake. His wings, which were of no use in the air, sustained him in the water, and the prince drew him to land, half dead with terror and vexation.

The Prince finds a Man of Learning

7 THE prince was not much afflicted by this disaster, having suffered himself to hope for a happier event, only because he had no other means of escape in view. He still persisted in his design to leave the happy valley by the first opportunity.

His imagination was now at a stand; he had no prospect of entering into the world; and, notwithstanding all his endeavors to support himself, discontent by degrees preyed upon him, and he began again to lose his thoughts in sadness, when the rainy season, which in these countries is periodical, made it inconvenient to wander in the woods.

The rain continued longer and with more violence than had been ever known; the clouds broke on the surrounding mountains, and the torrents streamed into the plain on every side, till the cavern was too narrow to discharge the water.

The lake overflowed its banks, and all the level of the valley was covered with the inundation. The eminence on which the palace was built and some other spots of rising ground were all that the eye could now discover. The herds and flocks left the pastures, and both the wild beasts and the tame retreated to the mountains.

This inundation confined all the princes to domestic amusements, and the attention of Rasselas was particularly seized by a poem, which Imlac rehearsed, upon the various conditions of humanity. He commanded the poet to attend him in his apartment and recite his verses a second time; then, entering into familiar talk, he thought himself happy in having found a man who knew the world so well and could so skilfully paint the scenes of life. He asked a thousand questions about things to which, though common to all other mortals, his confinement from childhood had kept him a stranger. The poet pitied his ignorance, and loved his curiosity, and entertained him from day to day with novelty and instruction, so that the prince regretted the necessity of sleep, and longed till the morning should renew his pleasure.

As they were sitting together, the prince commanded Imlac to relate his history and to tell by what accident he was forced, or by what motive induced, to close his life in the happy valley. As he was going to begin his narrative, Rasselas was called to a concert, and obliged to restrain his curiosity till the evening.

The History of Imlac

8   THE close of the day is, in the regions of
the torrid zone, the only season of diversion and entertainment, and it was therefore mid-
night before the music ceased and the princesses
retired. Rasselas then called for his companion,
and required him to begin the story of his life.

"Sir," said Imlac, "my history will not be long:
the life that is devoted to knowledge passes silently away and is very little diversified by events.
To talk in public, to think in solitude, to read and
to hear, to inquire and answer inquiries, is the
business of a scholar. He wanders about the world
without pomp or terror, and is neither known nor
valued but by men like himself.

"I was born in the kingdom of Goiama, at no
great distance from the fountain of the Nile. My
father was a wealthy merchant, who traded between the inland countries of Africk and the ports
of the Red Sea. He was honest, frugal, and diligent,
but of mean sentiments and narrow comprehension; he desired only to be rich and to conceal his

riches, lest he should be spoiled by the governors of the province."

"Surely," said the prince, "my father must be negligent of his charge, if any man in his dominions dares take that which belongs to another. Does he not know that kings are accountable for injustice permitted as well as done? If I were emperor, not the meanest of my subjects should be oppressed with impunity. My blood boils when I am told that a merchant durst not enjoy his honest gains for fear of losing them by rapacity of power. Name the governor who robbed the people, that I may declare his crimes to the emperor."

"Sir," said Imlac, "your ardor is the natural effect of virtue animated by youth; the time will come when you will acquit your father, and perhaps hear with less impatience of the governor. Oppression is, in the Abyssinian dominions, neither frequent nor tolerated; but no form of government has been yet discovered, by which cruelty can be wholly prevented. Subordination supposes power on one part and subjection on the other; and, if power be in the hands of men, it will sometimes be abused. The vigilance of the supreme magistrate may do much, but much will still remain undone. He can never know all the crimes that are committed, and can seldom punish all that he knows."

"This," said the prince, "I do not understand; but I had rather hear thee than dispute. Continue thy narration."

"My father," proceeded Imlac, "orginally intended that I should have no other education than such as might qualify me for commerce, and, discovering in me great strength of memory and quickness of apprehension, often declared his hope that I should become sometime the richest man in Abyssinia."

"Why," said the prince, "did thy father desire the increase of his wealth, when it was already greater than he durst discover or enjoy? I am unwilling to doubt thy veracity, yet inconsistencies cannot both be true."

"Inconsistencies," answered Imlac, "cannot both be right, but, imputed to man, they may both be true. Yet diversity is not inconsistency. My father might expect a time of greater security. However, some desire is necessary to keep life in motion, and he whose real wants are supplied must admit those of fancy."

"This," said the prince, "I can in some measure conceive. I repent that I interrupted thee."

"With this hope," proceeded Imlac, "he sent me to school, but, when I had once found the delight of knowledge, and felt the pleasure of intelligence and the pride of invention, I began silently to despise riches, and determined to disappoint the purpose of my father, whose grossness of conception raised my pity. I was twenty years old before his tenderness would expose me to the fatigue of travel, in which time I had been instructed by successive masters in all the literature of my native country. As every hour taught me something new, I lived in a continual course of gratification; but, as I advanced towards manhood, I lost much of the reverence with which I had been used to look on my instructors, because, when the lesson was ended, I did not find them wiser or better than common men.

"At length my father resolved to initiate me in commerce, and, opening one of his subterranean treasuries, counted out ten thousand pieces of gold. 'This, young man,' said he, 'is the stock with which you must negotiate. I began with less than the fifth, and you see how diligence and parsimony have increased it. This is your own to waste or to improve. If you squander it by negligence or caprice, you must wait for my death before you will be rich; if in four years you double your stock, we will thenceforward let subordination cease, and live together as friends and partners; for he shall always be equal with me, who is equally skilled in the art of growing rich.'

"We laid our money upon camels, concealed in bales of cheap goods, and travelled to the shore of the Red Sea. When I cast my eye on the expanse of waters, my heart bounded like that of a prisoner escaped. I felt an unextinguishable curiosity kindle in my mind, and resolved to snatch this opportunity of seeing the manners of other nations and of learning sciences unknown in Abyssinia.

"I remembered that my father had obliged me to the improvement of my stock, not by a promise I ought not to violate, but by a penalty which I was at liberty to incur, and therefore determined to gratify my predominant desire and, by drinking at the fountains of knowledge, to quench the thirst of curiosity.

"As I was supposed to trade without connection

with my father, it was easy for me to become acquainted with the master of a ship and procure a passage to some other country. I had no motives of choice to regulate my voyage; it was sufficient for me that, wherever I wandered, I should see a country which I had not seen before. I therefore entered a ship bound for Surat, having left a letter for my father declaring my intention.

The History of Imlac Continued

9 "WHEN I first entered upon the world of waters and lost sight of land, I looked round about me with pleasing terror, and, thinking my soul enlarged by the boundless prospect, imagined that I could gaze round for ever without satiety; but in a short time I grew weary of looking on barren uniformity, where I could only see again what I had already seen. I then descended into the ship and doubted for a while whether all my future pleasures would not end like this, in disgust and disappointment. Yet surely, said I, the ocean and the land are very different; the only variety of water is rest and motion, but the earth has mountains and valleys, deserts and cities; it is inhabited by men of different customs and contrary opinions; and I may hope to find variety in life, though I should miss it in nature.

"With this thought I quieted my mind, and amused myself during the voyage, sometimes by learning from the sailors the art of navigation, which I have never practiced, and sometimes by forming schemes for my conduct in different situations, in not one of which I have been ever placed.

"I was almost weary of my naval amusements when we landed safely at Surat. I secured my money, and, purchasing some commodities for show, joined myself to a caravan that was passing into the inland country. My companions, for some reason or other, conjecturing that I was rich, and, by my inquiries and admiration, finding that I was ignorant, considered me as a novice whom they had a right to cheat and who was to learn at the usual expense the art of fraud. They exposed me to the theft of servants and the exaction of officers, and saw me plundered upon false pretenses, without any advantage to themselves but that of rejoicing in the superiority of their own knowledge."

"Stop a moment," said the prince. "Is there such depravity in man as that he should injure another without benefit to himself? I can easily conceive that all are pleased with superiority, but your ignorance was merely accidental, which, being neither your crime nor your folly, could afford them no reason to applaud themselves; and the knowledge which they had, and which you had wanted, they might as effectually have shown by warning as betraying you."

"Pride," said Imlac, "is seldom delicate. It will please itself with very mean advantages, and envy feels not its own happiness but when it may be compared with the misery of others. They were my enemies because they grieved to think me rich, and my oppressors because they delighted to find me weak.''

"Proceed," said the prince. "I doubt not of the facts which you relate, but imagine that you impute them to mistaken motives.''

"In this company," said Imlac, "I arrived at Agra, the capital of Indostan, the city in which the great Mogul commonly resides. I applied myself to the language of the country and in a few months was able to converse with the learned men, some of whom I found morose and reserved, and others easy and communicative; some were unwilling to teach another what they had with difficulty learned themselves, and some showed that the end of their studies was to gain the dignity of instructing.

"To the tutor of the young princes I recommended myself so much that I was presented to the emperor as a man of uncommon knowledge. The emperor asked me many questions concerning my country and my travels, and, though I cannot now recollect anything that he uttered above the power of a common man, he dismissed me astonished at his wisdom and enamored of his goodness.

"My credit was now so high that the merchants with whom I had travelled applied to me for recommendations to the ladies of the court. I was surprised at their confidence of solicitation and gently reproached them with their practices on the road. They heard me with cold indifference and showed no tokens of shame or sorrow.

"They then urged their request with the offer

of a bribe, but what I would not do for kindness, I would not do for money, and refused them, not because they had injured me, but because I would not enable them to injure others; for I knew they would have made use of my credit to cheat those who should buy their wares.

"Having resided at Agra till there was no more to be learned, I travelled into Persia, where I saw many remains of ancient magnificence and observed many new accommodations of life. The Persians are a nation eminently social, and their assemblies afforded me daily opportunities of remarking characters and manners, and of tracing human nature through all its variations.

"From Persia I passed into Arabia, where I saw a nation at once pastoral and warlike, who live without any settled habitation, whose only wealth is their flocks and herds, and who have yet carried on through all ages an hereditary war with all mankind, though they neither covet nor envy their possessions.

Imlac's History Continued.
A Dissertation upon Poetry

10 "WHEREVER I went, I found that poetry was considered as the highest learning and regarded with a veneration somewhat approaching to that which man would pay to the angelic nature. And yet it fills me with wonder that, in almost all countries, the most ancient poets are considered as the best, whether it be that every other kind of knowledge is an acquisition gradually attained and poetry is a gift conferred at once; or that the first poetry of every nation surprised them as a novelty and retained the credit by consent, which it received by accident at first; or whether, as the province of poetry is to describe nature and passion, which are always the same, the first writers took possession of the most striking objects for description and the most probable occurrences for fiction, and left nothing to those that followed them but transcription of the same events and new combinations of the same im-

ages. Whatever be the reason, it is commonly observed that the early writers are in possession of nature, and their followers of art; that the first excel in strength and invention, and the latter in elegance and refinement.

"I was desirous to add my name to this illustrious fraternity. I read all the poets of Persia and Arabia, and was able to repeat by memory the volumes that are suspended in the mosque of Mecca. But I soon found that no man was ever great by imitation. My desire of excellence impelled me to transfer my attention to nature and to life. Nature was to be my subject, and men to be my auditors. I could never describe what I had not seen; I could not hope to move those with delight or terror, whose interests and opinions I did not understand.

"Being now resolved to be a poet, I saw everything with a new purpose; my sphere of attention was suddenly magnified; no kind of knowledge was to be overlooked. I ranged mountains and deserts for images and resemblances, and pictured upon my mind every tree of the forest and flower of the valley. I observed with equal care the crags of the rock and the pinnacles of the palace. Sometimes I wandered along the mazes of the rivulet, and sometimes watched the changes of the summer clouds. To a poet nothing can be useless. Whatever is beautiful, and whatever is dreadful, must be familiar to his imagination; he must be conversant with all that is awfully vast or elegantly little. The plants of the garden, the animals of the wood, the minerals of the earth, and meteors of the sky, must all concur to store his mind with inexhaust-

ible variety, for every idea is useful for the enforce-
ment or decoration of moral or religious truth; and
he who knows most will have most power of di-
versifying his scenes and of gratifying his reader
with remote allusions and unexpected instruction.

"All the appearances of nature I was therefore
careful to study, and every country which I have
surveyed has contributed something to my political
powers."

"In so wide a survey," said the prince, "you
must surely have left much unobserved. I have
lived, till now, within the circuit of these mountains, and yet cannot walk abroad without the
sight of something which I had never beheld before or never heeded."

"The business of a poet," said Imlac, "is to
examine not the individual, but the species; to
remark general properties and large appearances.
He does not number the streaks of the tulip, or
describe the different shades in the verdure of the
forest; he is to exhibit in his portraits of nature
such prominent and striking features as recall the
original to every mind, and must neglect the mi-
nuter discriminations, which one may have remarked and another have neglected, for those
characteristics which are alike obvious to vigilance
and carelessness.

"But the knowledge of nature is only half the
task of a poet; he must be acquainted likewise
with all the modes of life. His character requires
that he estimate the happiness and misery of every
condition, and trace the changes of the human
mind as they are modified by various institutions

and accidental influences of climate or custom, from the sprightliness of infancy to the despondence of decrepitude. He must divest himself of the prejudices of his age and country; he must consider right and wrong in present laws and opinions, and rise to general and transcendental truths, which will always be the same. He must therefore content himself with the slow progress of his name, contemn the applause of his own time, and commit his claims to the justice of posterity. He must write as the interpreter of nature, and the legislator of mankind, and consider himself as presiding over the thoughts and manners of future generations, as a being superior to time and place.

"His labor is not yet at an end; he must know many languages and many sciences; and, that his style may be worthy of his thoughts, must, by incessant practice, familiarize to himself every delicacy of speech and grace of harmony."

Imlac's Narrative Continued.
A Hint on Pilgrimage

I I   IMLAC now felt the enthusiastic fit, and was proceeding to aggrandize his own profession, when the prince cried out, "Enough! Thou hast convinced me that no human being can ever be a poet. Proceed with thy narration."

"To be a poet," said Imlac, "is indeed very difficult."

"So difficult," returned the prince, "that I will at present hear no more of his labors. Tell me whither you went when you had seen Persia."

"From Persia," said the poet, "I travelled through Syria, and for three years resided in Palestine, where I conversed with great numbers of the northern and western nations of Europe, the nations which are now in possession of all power and all knowledge, whose armies are irresistible and whose fleets command the remotest parts of the globe. When I compared these men with the natives of our own kingdom and those that surround us, they appeared almost another order of beings. In their countries it is difficult to wish for anything that may not be obtained. A thousand arts, of which we never heard, are continually laboring for their convenience and pleasure, and whatever their own climate has denied them is supplied by their commerce."

"By what means," said the prince, "are the Europeans thus powerful, or why, since they can so easily visit Asia and Africa for trade or conquest, cannot the Asiatics and Africans invade their coasts, plant colonies in their ports, and give laws to their natural princes? The same wind that carries them back would bring us thither."

"They are more powerful, sir, than we," answered Imlac, "because they are wiser. Knowledge will always predominate over ignorance, as man governs the other animals. But why their knowledge is more than ours, I know not what reason can be given, but the unsearchable will of the Supreme Being."

"When," said the prince with a sigh, "shall I be able to visit Palestine and mingle with this mighty confluence of nations? Till that happy moment shall arrive, let me fill up the time with such representations as thou canst give me. I am not ignorant of the motive that assembles such numbers in that place, and cannot but consider it as the center of wisdom and piety, to which the best and wisest men of every land must be continually resorting."

"There are some nations," said Imlac, "that send few visitants to Palestine, for many numerous and learned sects in Europe concur to censure pilgrimage as superstitious or deride it as ridiculous."

"You know," said the prince, "how little my life has made me acquainted with diversity of opinions; it will be too long to hear the arguments on both sides; you, that have considered them, tell me the result."

"Pilgrimage," said Imlac, "like many other acts of piety, may be reasonable or superstitious, according to the principles upon which it is performed. Long journeys in search of truth are not commanded. Truth, such as is necessary to the regulation of life, is always found where it is honestly sought. Change of place is no natural cause of the increase of piety, for it inevitably produces dissipation of mind. Yet, since men go every day to view the fields where great actions have been performed and return with stronger impressions of the event, curiosity of the same kind may naturally dispose us to view that country whence our religion had its beginning; and I believe no man surveys those awful scenes without some confirmation of holy resolutions. That the Supreme Being may be more easily propitiated in one place than in another, is the dream of idle superstition; but that some places may operate upon our own minds in an uncommon manner, is an opinion which hourly experience will justify. He who supposes that his vices may be more successfully combated in Palestine will, perhaps, find himself mistaken; yet he may go thither without folly. He who thinks they will be more freely pardoned dishonors at once his reason and religion."

"These," said the prince, "are European distinctions. I will consider them another time. What have you found to be the effect of knowledge? Are those nations happier than we?"

"There is so much infelicity," said the poet, "in the world, that scarce any man has leisure from his own distresses to estimate the comparative happiness of others. Knowledge is certainly one of the means of pleasure, as is confessed by the natural desire which every mind feels of increasing its ideas. Ignorance is mere privation, by which nothing can be produced; it is a vacuity in which the soul sits motionless and torpid for want of attraction, and, without knowing why, we always rejoice when we learn and grieve when we forget. I am therefore inclined to conclude that, if nothing counteracts the natural consequence of learning, we grow more happy as our minds take a wider range.

"In enumerating the particular comforts of life, we shall find many advantages on the side of the Europeans. They cure wounds and diseases with which we languish and perish. We suffer inclemencies of weather which they can obviate. They have engines for the dispatch of many laborious works which we must perform by manual industry. There is such communication between distant places that one friend can hardly be said to be absent from another. Their policy removes all public inconveniences; they have roads cut through their mountains and bridges laid upon their rivers. And, if we descend to the privacies of life, their habitations are more commodious, and their possessions are more secure."

"They are surely happy," said the prince, "who have all these conveniences, of which I envy none so much as the facility with which separated friends interchange their thoughts."

"The Europeans," answered Imlac, "are less unhappy than we; but they are not happy. Human life is everywhere a state in which much is to be endured, and little to be enjoyed."

The Story of Imlac Continued

12 "I am not yet willing," said the prince, "to suppose that happiness is so parsimoniously distributed to mortals; nor can believe but that, if I had the choice of life, I should be able to fill every day with pleasure. I would injure no man, and should provoke no resentment; I would relieve every distress, and should enjoy the benedictions of gratitude. I would choose my friends among the wise, and my wife among the virtuous; and therefore should be in no danger from treachery or unkindness. My children should, by my care, be learned and pious, and would repay to my age what their childhood had received. What would dare to molest him who might call on every side to thousands enriched by his bounty or assisted by his power? And why should not life glide quietly away in the soft reciprocation of protection and reverence? All this may be done without the help of European refinements, which appear by their effects to be rather specious than useful. Let us leave them, and pursue our journey."

"From Palestine," said Imlac, "I passed through many regions of Asia, in the more civilized kingdoms as a trader and among the barbarians of the mountains as a pilgrim. At last I began to long for my native country, that I might repose, after my travels and fatigues, in the places where I had spent my earliest years and gladden my old companions with the recital of my adventures. Often did I figure to myself those with whom I had sported away the gay hours of dawning life, sitting round me in its evening, wondering at my tales, and listening to my counsels.

"When this thought had taken possession of my mind, I considered every moment as wasted which did not bring me nearer to Abyssinia. I hastened into Egypt and, notwithstanding my impatience, was detained ten months in the contemplation of its ancient magnificence and in inquiries after the remains of its ancient learning. I found in Cairo a mixture of all nations, some brought thither by the love of knowledge, some by the hope of gain, and many by the desire of living after their own manner without observation and of lying hid in the obscurity of multitudes; for in a city populous as Cairo, it is possible to obtain at the same time the gratifications of society and secrecy of solitude.

"From Cairo I travelled to Suez, and embarked on the Red Sea, passing along the coast till I arrived at the port from which I had departed twenty years before. Here I joined myself to a caravan and re-entered my native country.

"I now expected the caresses of my kinsmen and

the congratulations of my friends, and was not without hope that my father, whatever value he had set upon riches, would own with gladness and pride a son who was able to add to the felicity and honor of the nation. But I was soon convinced that my thoughts were vain. My father had been dead fourteen years, having divided his wealth among my brothers, who were removed to some other provinces. Of my companions, the greater part were in the grave; of the rest, some could with difficulty remember me, and some considered me as one corrupted by foreign manners.

"A man used to vicissitudes is not easily dejected. I forgot, after a time, my disappointment, and endeavored to recommend myself to the nobles of the kingdom. They admitted me to their tables, heard my story, and dismissed me. I opened a school, and was prohibited to teach. I then resolved to sit down in the quiet of domestic life, and addressed a lady that was fond of my conversation, but rejected my suit because my father was a merchant.

"Wearied at last with solicitation and repulses, I resolved to hide myself forever from the world, and depend no longer on the opinion or caprice of others. I waited for the time when the gate of the *happy valley* should open, that I might bid farewell to hope and fear. The day came. My performance was distinguished with favor, and I resigned myself with joy to perpetual confinement."

"Hast thou here found happiness at last?" said Rasselas. "Tell me without reserve. Art thou content with thy condition? Or dost thou wish to be again wandering and inquiring? All the inhabitants of this valley celebrate their lot and, at the annual visit of the emperor, invite others to partake of their felicity."

"Great prince," said Imlac, "I shall speak the truth. I know not one of all your attendants, who does not lament the hour when he entered this retreat. I am less unhappy than the rest, because I have a mind replete with images, which I can vary and combine at pleasure. I can amuse my solitude by the renovation of the knowledge which begins to fade from my memory and by recollection of the incidents of my past life. Yet all this ends in the sorrowful consideration that my acquirements are now useless and that none of my pleasures can be again enjoyed. The rest, whose minds have no impression but of the present moment, are either corroded by malignant passions or sit stupid in the gloom of perpetual vacancy."

"What passions can infest those," said the prince, "who have no rivals? We are in a place where impotence precludes malice and where all envy is repressed by community of enjoyments."

"There may be community," said Imlac, "of material possessions, but there can never be community of love or of esteem. It must happen that one will please more than another; he that knows himself despised will always be envious; and still more envious and malevolent, if he is condemned to live in the presence of those who despise him. The invitations, by which they allure others to a state which they feel to be wretched, proceed from the natural malignity of hopeless misery.

They are weary of themselves and of each other, and expect to find relief in new companions. They envy the liberty which their folly has forfeited, and would gladly see all mankind imprisoned like themselves.

"From this crime, however, I am wholly free. No man can say that he is wretched by my persuasion. I look with pity on the crowds who are annually soliciting admission to captivity, and wish that it were lawful for me to warn them of their danger."

"My dear Imlac," said the prince, "I will open to thee my whole heart. I have long meditated an escape from the *happy valley*. I have examined the mountains on every side, but find myself insuperably barred. Teach me the way to break my prison. Thou shalt be the companion of my flight, the guide of my rambles, the partner of my fortune, and my sole director in the *choice of life*."

"Sir," answered the poet, "your escape will be difficult, and, perhaps, you may soon repent your curiosity. The world, which you figure to yourself smooth and quiet as the lake in the valley, you will find a sea foaming with tempests and boiling with whirlpools; you will be sometimes overwhelmed by the waves of violence, and sometimes dashed against the rocks of treachery. Amidst wrongs and frauds, competitions and anxieties, you will wish a thousand times for these seats of quiet, and willingly quit hope to be free from fear."

"Do not seek to deter me from my purpose," said the prince. "I am impatient to see what thou hast seen, and, since thou art thyself weary of the valley, it is evident that thy former state was better than this. Whatever be the consequence of my experiment, I am resolved to judge with mine own eyes of the various conditions of men, and then to make deliberately my *choice of life*."

"I am afraid," said Imlac, "you are hindered by stronger restraints than my persuasions; yet, if your determination is fixed, I do not counsel you to despair. Few things are impossible to diligence and skill."

Rasselas Discovers the Means of Escape

13 ❦ THE prince now dismissed his favorite to rest, but the narrative of wonders and novelties filled his mind with perturbation. He revolved all that he had heard and prepared innumerable questions for the morning.

Much of his uneasiness was now removed. He had a friend to whom he could impart his thoughts and whose experience could assist him in all his designs. His heart was no longer condemned to swell with silent vexation. He thought that even the *happy valley* might be endured with such a companion and that, if they could range the world together, he should have nothing further to desire.

In a few days the water was discharged, and the ground dried. The prince and Imlac then walked out together, to converse without the notice of the rest. The prince, whose thoughts were always on the wing, as he passed by the gate, said with a countenance of sorrow, "Why art thou so strong, and why is man so weak?"

"Man is not weak," answered his companion.

"Knowledge is more than equivalent to force. The master of mechanics laughs at strength. I can burst the gate, but cannot do it secretly. Some other expedient must be tried."

As they were walking on the side of the mountain, they observed that the coneys, which the rain had driven from their burrows, had taken shelter among the bushes and formed holes behind them, tending upwards in an oblique line. "It has been the opinion of antiquity," said Imlac, "that human reason borrowed many arts from the instinct of animals; let us, therefore, not think ourselves degraded by learning from the coney. We may escape by piercing the mountain in the same direction. We will begin where the summit hangs over the middle part, and labor upward till we shall issue up beyond the prominence."

The eyes of the prince, when he heard this proposal, sparkled with joy. The execution was easy, and the success certain.

No time was now lost. They hastened early in the morning to choose a place proper for their mine. They clambered with great fatigue among crags and brambles, and returned without having discovered any part that favored their design. The second and the third day were spent in the same manner, and with the same frustration. But, on the fourth, they found a small cavern, concealed by a thicket, where they resolved to make their experiment.

Imlac procured instruments proper to hew stone and remove earth, and they fell to their work on the next day with more eagerness than vigor. They were presently exhausted by their efforts, and sat down to pant upon the grass. The prince, for a moment, appeared to be discouraged. "Sir," said his companion, "practice will enable us to continue our labor for a longer time. Mark, however, how far we have advanced, and you will find that our toil will some time have an end. Great works are performed, not by strength, but perseverance; yonder palace was raised by single stones, yet you see its height and spaciousness. He that shall walk with vigor three hours a day will pass in seven years a space equal to the circumference of the globe."

They returned to their work day after day, and, in a short time, found a fissure in the rock, which enabled them to pass far with very little obstruction. This Rasselas considered as a good omen. "Do not disturb your mind," said Imlac, "with other hopes or fears than reason may suggest. If you are pleased with prognostics of good, you will be terrified likewise with tokens of evil, and your whole life will be a prey to superstition. Whatever facilitates our work is more than an omen; it is a cause of success. This is one of those pleasing surprises which often happen to active resolution. Many things difficult to design prove easy to performance."

Rasselas and Imlac Receive
an Unexpected Visit

14   **THEY** had now wrought their way to the middle, and solaced their toil with the approach of liberty, when the prince, coming down to refresh himself with air, found his sister Nekayah standing before the mouth of the cavity. He started and stood confused, afraid to tell his design, and yet hopeless to conceal it. A few moments determined him to repose on her fidelity, and secure her secrecy by a declaration without reserve.

"Do not imagine," said the princess, "that I came hither as a spy. I had long observed from my window that you and Imlac directed your walk every day towards the same point; but I did not suppose that you had any better reason for the preference than a cooler shade, or more fragrant bank, nor followed you with any other design than to partake of your conversation. Since, then, not suspicion but fondness has detected you, let me not lose the advantage of my discovery. I am equally weary of confinement with yourself and not less desirous of knowing what is done or suffered in the world. Permit me to fly with you from this tasteless tranquillity, which will yet grow more loathsome when you have left me. You may deny me to accompany you, but cannot hinder me from following."

The prince, who loved Nekayah above his other sisters, had no inclination to refuse her request, and grieved that he had lost an opportunity of showing his confidence by a voluntary communication. It was therefore agreed that she should leave the valley with them and that, in the meantime, she should watch lest any other straggler should, by chance or curiosity, follow them to the mountain.

At length their labor was at an end. They saw light beyond the prominence and, issuing to the top of the mountain, beheld the Nile, yet a narrow current, wandering beneath them.

The prince looked round with rapture, anticipated all the pleasure of travel, and in thought was already transported beyond his father's dominions. Imlac, though very joyful at his escape, had less expectation of pleasure in the world, which he had before tried and of which he had been weary.

Rasselas was so much delighted with a wider horizon that he could not soon be persuaded to return into the valley. He informed his sister that the way was open and that nothing now remained but to prepare for their departure.

The Prince and the Princess
Leave the Valley and See
Many Wonders

15 AS THE prince and princess had jewels sufficient to make them rich, whenever they came into a place of commerce, which, by Imlac's direction, they hid in their clothes; and, on the night of the next full moon, all left the valley. The princess was followed only by a single favorite, who did not know whither she was going.

They clambered through the cavity, and began to go down on the other side. The princess and her maid turned their eyes towards every part, and, seeing nothing to bound their prospect, considered themselves as in danger of being lost in a dreary vacuity. They stopped and trembled. "I am almost afraid," said the princess, "to begin a journey of which I cannot perceive an end, and to venture into this immense plain, where I may be approached on every side by men whom I never saw." The prince felt nearly the same emotions, though he thought it more manly to conceal them.

Imlac smiled at their terrors and encouraged them to proceed, but the princess continued irresolute till she had been imperceptibly drawn forward too far to return.

In the morning they found some shepherds in the field, who set milk and fruits before them. The princess wondered that she did not see a palace ready for her reception, and a table spread with delicacies; but, being faint and hungry, she drank the milk and ate the fruits, and thought them of a higher flavor than the products of the valley.

They travelled forward by easy journeys, being all unaccustomed to toil or difficulty, and knowing that, though they might be missed, they could not be pursued. In a few days they came into a more populous region, where Imlac was diverted with the admiration which his companions expressed at the diversity of manners, stations, and employments.

Their dress was such as might not bring upon them the suspicion of having anything to conceal, yet the prince, wherever he came, expected to be obeyed, and the princess was frightened because those that came into her presence did not prostrate themselves before her. Imlac was forced to observe them with great vigilance, lest they should betray their rank by their unusual behavior, and detained them several weeks in the first village, to accustom them to the sight of common mortals.

By degrees the royal wanderers were taught to understand that they had for a time laid aside their dignity, and were to expect only such regard as liberality and courtesy could procure. And Imlac, having by many admonitions prepared them to endure the tumults of a port and the ruggedness of the commercial race, brought them down to the seacoast.

The prince and his sister, to whom everything was new, were gratified equally at all places, and therefore remained for some months at the port, without any inclination to pass further. Imlac was content with their stay, because he did not think it safe to expose them, unpracticed in the world, to the hazards of a foreign country.

At last he began to fear lest they should be discovered, and proposed to fix a day for their departure. They had no pretensions to judge for themselves, and referred the whole scheme to his direction. He therefore took passage in a ship to Suez, and, when the time came, with great difficulty prevailed on the princess to enter the vessel. They had a quick and prosperous voyage, and from Suez travelled by land to Cairo.

They Enter Cairo and Find Every Man Happy

16 AS they approached the city, which filled the strangers with astonishment, "This," said Imlac to the prince, "is the place where travellers and merchants assemble from all the corners of the earth. You will here find men of every character, and every occupation. Commerce is here honorable; I will act as a merchant, and you shall live as strangers who have no other end of travel than curiosity. It will soon be observed that we are rich; our reputation will procure us access to all whom we shall desire to know; you will see all the conditions of humanity, and enable yourself at leisure to make your *choice of life*."

They now entered the town, stunned by the noise and offended by the crowds. Instruction had not yet so prevailed over habit but that they wondered to see themselves pass undistinguished along the street and met by the lowest of the people without reverence or notice. The princess could not at first bear the thought of being levelled with the vulgar, and for some days continued in her chamber, where she was served by her favorite Pekuah as in the palace of the valley.

Imlac, who understood traffic, sold part of the jewels the next day and hired a house, which he adorned with such magnificence that he was immediately considered as a merchant of great wealth. His politeness attracted many acquaintance, and his generosity made him courted by many dependents. His table was crowded by men of every nation, who all admired his knowledge and solicited his favor. His companions, not being able to mix in the conversation, could make no discovery of their ignorance or surprise, and were gradually initiated in the world as they gained knowledge of the language.

The prince had, by frequent lectures, been taught the use and nature of money; but the ladies could not, for a long time, comprehend what the merchants did with small pieces of gold and silver, or why things of so little use should be received as equivalent to the necessaries of life.

They studied the language two years, while Imlac was preparing to set before them the various ranks and conditions of mankind. He grew acquainted with all who had anything uncommon in their fortune or conduct. He frequented the voluptuous and the frugal, the idle and the busy, the merchants and the men of learning.

The prince, being now able to converse with fluency and having learned the caution necessary to be observed in his intercourse with strangers, began to accompany Imlac to places of resort and to enter into all assemblies, that he might make his *choice of life*.

For some time he thought choice needless, because all appeared to him equally happy. Whereever he went, he met gaiety and kindness, and heard the song of joy or the laugh of carelessness. He began to believe that the world overflowed with universal plenty and that nothing was withheld either from want or merit, that every hand showered liberality and every heart melted with benevolence. "And who then," says he, " will be suffered to be wretched?"

Imlac permitted the pleasing delusion and was unwilling to crush the hope of inexperience, till, one day, having sat a while silent, "I know not," said the prince, "what can be the reason that I am more unhappy than any of our friends. I see them perpetually and unalterably cheerful, but feel my own mind restless and uneasy. I am unsatisfied with those pleasures which I seem most to court. I live in the crowds of jollity, not so much to enjoy company as to shun myself, and am only loud and merry to conceal my sadness."

"Every man," said Imlac, "may, by examining his own mind, guess what passes in the minds of others. When you feel that your own gaiety is counterfeit, it may justly lead you to suspect that of your companions not to be sincere. Envy is commonly reciprocal. We are long before we are convinced that happiness is never to be found, and each believes it possessed by others, to keep alive the hope of obtaining it for himself. In the assembly where you passed the last night, there appeared such sprightliness of air and volatility of fancy as might have suited beings of a higher order, formed to inhabit serener regions inaccessible to care or sorrow. Yet, believe me, prince, there was not one who did not dread the moment when solitude should deliver him to the tyranny of reflection."

"This," said the prince, "may be true of others, since it is true of me; yet, whatever be the general infelicity of man, one condition is more happy than another, and wisdom surely directs us to take the least evil in the *choice of life*."

"The causes of good and evil," answered Imlac, "are so various and uncertain, so often entangled with each other, so diversified by various relations, and so much subject to accidents which cannot be foreseen, that he who would fix his condition upon incontestable reasons of preference must live and die inquiring and deliberating."

"But surely," said Rasselas, "the wise men, to whom we listen with reverence and wonder, chose that mode of life for themselves which they thought most likely to make them happy."

"Very few," said the poet, "live by choice. Every man is placed in his present condition by causes which acted without his foresight and with which he did not always willingly cooperate; and therefore you will rarely meet one who does not think the lot of his neighbor better than his own."

"I am pleased to think," said the prince, "that my birth has given me at least one advantage over others, by enabling me to determine for myself. I have here the world before me; I will review it at leisure. Surely happiness is somewhere to be found."

The Prince Associates with Young Men of Spirit and Gaiety

17 RASSELAS rose next day and resolved to begin his experiments upon life. "Youth," cried he, "is the time of gladness. I will join myself to the young men whose only business is to gratify their desires and whose time is all spent in a succession of enjoyments."

To such societies he was readily admitted, but a few days brought him back weary and disgusted. Their mirth was without images, their laughter without motive; their pleasures were gross and sensual, in which the mind had no part. Their conduct was at once wild and mean. They laughed at order and at law, but the frown of power dejected, and the eye of wisdom abashed them.

The prince soon concluded that he should never be happy in a course of life of which he was ashamed. He thought it unsuitable to a reasonable being to act without a plan, and to be sad or cheerful only by chance. "Happiness," said he, "must be something solid and permanent, without fear and without uncertainty."

But his young companions had gained so much of his regard by their frankness and courtesy that he could not leave them without warning and remonstrance. "My friends," said he, "I have seriously considered our manners and our prospects, and find that we have mistaken our own interest. The first years of man must make provision for the last. He that never thinks never can be wise. Perpetual levity must end in ignorance, and intemperance, though it may fire the spirits for an hour, will make life short or miserable. Let us consider that youth is of no long duration and that in maturer age, when the enchantments of fancy shall cease and phantoms of delight dance no more about us, we shall have no comforts but the esteem of wise men and the means of doing good. Let us, therefore, stop, while to stop is in our power. Let us live as men who are some time to grow old and to whom it will be the most dreadful of all evils to count their past years by follies and to be reminded of their former luxuriance of health only by the maladies which riot has produced."

They stared a while in silence one upon another, and at last drove him away by a general chorus of continued laughter.

The consciousness that his sentiments were just, and his intentions kind, was scarcely sufficient to support him against the horror of derision. But he recovered his tranquillity and pursued his search.

The Prince finds a Wise and Happy Man

18   As he was one day walking in the street, he saw a spacious building, which all were, by the open doors, invited to enter. He followed the stream of people, and found it a hall or school of declamation, in which professors read lectures to their auditory. He fixed his eye upon a sage raised above the rest, who discoursed with great energy on the government of the passions. His look was venerable, his action graceful, his pronunciation clear, and his diction elegant. He showed, with great strength of sentiment and variety of illustration, that human nature is degraded and debased when the lower faculties predominate over the higher; that when fancy, the parent of passion, usurps the dominion of the mind, nothing ensues but the natural effect of unlawful government — perturbation and confusion; that she betrays the fortresses of the intellect to rebels and excites her children to sedition against reason, their lawful

sovereign. He compared reason to the sun, of which light is constant, uniform, and lasting; and fancy to a meteor, of bright but transitory lustre, irregular in its motion and delusive in its direction.

He then communicated the various precepts given from time to time for the conquest of passion, and displayed the happiness of those who had obtained the important victory, after which man is no longer the slave of fear, nor the fool of hope; is no more emaciated by envy, inflamed by anger, emasculated by tenderness, or depressed by grief, but walks on calmly through the tumults or privacies of life, as the sun pursues alike his course through the calm of the stormy sky.

He enumerated many examples of heroes immovable by pain or pleasure, who looked with indifference on those modes or accidents to which the vulgar give the names of good and evil. He exhorted his hearers to lay aside their prejudices, and arm themselves against the shafts of malice or misfortune, by invulnerable patience; concluding that this state only was happiness and that this happiness was in everyone's power.

Rasselas listened to him with the veneration due to the instructions of a superior being, and, waiting for him at the door, humbly implored the liberty of visiting so great a master of true wisdom. The lecturer hesitated a moment, when Rasselas put a purse of gold into his hand, which he received with a mixture of joy and wonder.

"I have found," said the prince at his return to Imlac, "a man who can teach all that is necessary to be known; who, from the unshaken throne of rational fortitude, looks down on the scenes of life changing beneath him. He speaks, and attention watches his lips; he reasons, and conviction closes his periods. This man shall be my future guide. I will learn his doctrines, and imitate his life."

"Be not too hasty," said Imlac, "to trust or to admire the teachers of morality. They discourse like angels, but they live like men."

Rasselas, who could not conceive how any man could reason so forcibly without feeling the cogency of his own arguments, paid his visit in a few days, and was denied admission. He had now learned the power of money, and made his way by a piece of gold to the inner apartment, where he found the philosopher, in a room half darkened, with his eyes misty and his face pale. "Sir," said he, "you are come at a time when all human friendship is useless. What I suffer cannot be remedied; what I have lost cannot be supplied. My daughter, my only daughter, from whose tenderness I expected all the comforts of my age, died last night of a fever. My views, my purposes, my hopes are at an end. I am now a lonely being, disunited from society."

"Sir," said the prince, "mortality is an event by which a wise man can never be surprised. We know that death is always near, and it should therefore always be expected."

"Young man," answered the philosopher, "you speak like one that has never felt the pangs of separation." "Have you then forgot the precepts," said Rasselas, "which you so powerfully enforced? Has wisdom no strength to arm the heart against calamity? Consider that external things are naturally variable, but truth and reason are always the same." "What comfort," said the mourner, "can truth and reason afford me? Of what effect are they now, but to tell me that my daughter will not be restored?"

The prince, whose humanity would not suffer him to insult misery with reproof, went away convinced of the emptiness of rhetorical sound, and the inefficacy of polished periods and studied sentences.

A Glimpse of Pastoral Life

19 HE was still eager upon the same inquiry; and having heard of a hermit that lived near the lowest cataract of the Nile and filled the whole country with the fame of his sanctity, resolved to visit his retreat and inquire whether that felicity, which public life could not afford, was to be found in solitude, and whether a man, whose age and virtue made him venerable, could teach any peculiar art of shunning evils or enduring them.

Imlac and the princess agreed to accompany him; and, after the necessary preparations, they began their journey. Their way lay through the fields, where shepherds tended their flocks, and the lambs were playing upon the pasture. "This," said the poet, "is the life which has been often celebrated for its innocence and quiet; let us pass the heat of the day among the shepherds' tents, and know whether all our searches are not to terminate in pastoral simplicity."

The proposal pleased them, and they induced the shepherds, by small presents and familiar questions, to tell their opinion of their own state. They were so rude and ignorant, so little able to compare the good with the evil of the occupation, and so indistinct in their narratives and descriptions, that very little could be learned from them. But it was evident that their hearts were cankered with discontent, that they considered themselves as condemned to labor for the luxury of the rich, and looked up with stupid malevolence toward those that were placed above them.

The princess pronounced with vehemence that she would never suffer these envious savages to be her companions and that she should not soon be desirous of seeing any more speciments of rustic happiness; but could not believe that all the accounts of primeval pleasures were fabulous, and was yet in doubt whether life had anything that could be justly preferred to the placid gratifications of fields and woods. She hoped that the time would come when, with a few virtuous and elegant companions, she should gather flowers planted by her own hand, fondle the lambs of her own ewe, and listen without care, among brooks and breezes, to one of her maidens reading in the shade.

The Danger of Prosperity

20 ❦ ON the next day they continued their journey, till the heat compelled them to look round for shelter. At a small distance they saw a thick wood, which they no sooner entered than they perceived that they were approaching the habitations of men. The shrubs were diligently cut away to open walks where the shades were darkest; the boughs of opposite trees were artificially interwoven; seats of flowery turf were raised in vacant spaces; and a rivulet, that wantoned along the side of a winding path, had its banks sometimes opened into small basins and its stream sometimes obstructed by little mounds of stone, heaped together to increase its murmurs.

They passed slowly through the wood, delighted with such unexpected accommodations, and entertained each other with conjecturing what or who he could be that, in those rude and unfrequented regions, had leisure and art for such harmless luxury.

As they advanced, they heard the sound of music,

and saw youths and virgins dancing in the grove, and, going still further, beheld a stately palace built upon a hill, surrounded with woods. The laws of eastern hospitality allowed them to enter, and the master welcomed them like a man liberal and wealthy.

He was skilful enough in appearances soon to discern that they were no common guests, and spread his table with magnificance. The eloquence of Imlac caught his attention, and the lofty courtesy of the princess excited his respect. When they offered to depart, he entreated their stay, and was the next day still more unwilling to dismiss them than before. They were easily persuaded to stop, and civility grew up in time to freedom and confidence.

The prince now saw all the domestics cheerful and all the face of nature smiling round the place, and could not forbear to hope he should find here what he was seeking; but, when he was congratulating the master upon his possessions, he answered with a sigh: "My condition has indeed the appearance of happiness, but appearances are delusive. My prosperity puts my life in danger; the Bassa of Egypt is my enemy, incensed only by my wealth and popularity. I have been hitherto protected against him by the princes of the country, but, as favor of the great is uncertain, I know not how soon my defenders may be persuaded to share the plunder with the Bassa. I have sent my treasures into a distant country, and, upon the first alarm, am prepared to follow them. Then will my enemies riot in my mansion, and enjoy the gardens which I have planted."

They all joined in lamenting his danger and deprecating his exile; and the princess was so much disturbed with the tumult of grief and indignation that she retired to her apartment.

They continued with their kind inviter a few days longer, and then went forward to find the hermit.

The Happiness of Solitude.
The Hermit's History

21   THEY came on the third day, by the direction of the peasants, to the hermit's cell. It was a cavern in the side of a mountain, overshadowed with palm trees, at such a distance from the cataract that nothing more was heard than a gentle uniform murmur such as composed the mind to pensive meditation, especially when it was assisted by the wind whistling among the branches. The first rude essay of nature had been so much improved by human labor that the cave contained several apartments appropriated to different uses and often afforded lodging to travellers whom darkness or tempests happened to overtake.

The hermit sat on a bench at the door, to enjoy the coolness of the evening. On one side lay a book with pens and papers, on the other mechanical instruments of various kinds. As they approached him unregarded, the princess observed that he had not the countenance of a man that had found or could teach the way to happiness.

They saluted him with great respect, which he repaid like a man not unaccustomed to the forms of courts. "My children," said he, "if you have lost your way, you shall be willingly supplied with such conveniences for the night as this cavern will afford. I have all that nature requires, and you will not expect delicacies in a hermit's cell."

They thanked him and, entering, were pleased with the neatness and regularity of the place. The hermit set flesh and wine before them, though he fed only upon fruits and water. His discourse was cheerful without levity and pious without enthusiasm. He soon gained the esteem of his guests, and the princess repented of her hasty censure.

At last Imlac began thus: "I do not now wonder that your reputation is so far extended. We have heard at Cairo of your wisdom, and came hither to implore your direction for this young man and maiden in the *choice of life*."

"To him that lives well," answered the hermit, "every form of life is good, nor can I give any other rule for choice than to remove from all apparent evil."

"He will remove most certainly from evil," said the prince, "who shall devote himself to that solitude which you have recommended by your example."

"I have indeed lived fifteen years in solitude," said the hermit, "but have no desire that my example should gain any imitators. In my youth I professed arms, and was raised by degrees to the highest military rank. I have traversed wide countries at the head of my troops, and seen many battles and sieges. At last, being disgusted by the preferments of a younger officer and feeling that my vigor was beginning to decay, I was resolved to close my life in peace, having found the world full of snares, discord, and misery. I had once escaped from the pursuit of the enemy by the shelter of this cavern, and therefore chose it for my final residence. I employed artificers to form it into chambers, and stored it with all that I was likely to want.

"For some time after my retreat, I rejoiced like a tempest-beaten sailor at his entrance into the harbor, being delighted with the sudden change of the noise and hurry of war to stillness and repose. When the pleasure of novelty went away, I employed my hours in examining the plants which grow in the valley and the minerals which I collected from the rocks. But that inquiry is now grown tasteless and irksome. I have been for some time unsettled and distracted. My mind is disturbed with a thousand perplexities of doubt and vanities of imagination, which hourly prevail upon me, because I have no opportunities of relaxation or diversion. I am sometimes ashamed to think that I could not secure myself from vice, but by retiring from the exercise of virtue, and begin to suspect that I was rather impelled by resentment, than led by devotion, into solitude. My fancy riots in scenes of folly, and I lament that I have lost so much and have gained so little. In solitude, if I escape the example of bad men, I want likewise the counsel and conversation of the good. I have been long comparing the evils with the advantages of society, and resolve to return into the world tomorrow. The life of a solitary man will be certainly miserable, but not certainly devout."

They heard his resolution with surprise, but after a short pause offered to conduct him to Cairo. He dug up a considerable treasure, which he had hid among the rocks, and accompanied them to the city, on which, as he approached it, he gazed with rapture.

The Happiness of a Life
Led According to Nature

22 RASSELAS went often to an assembly of learned men who met at stated times to unbend their minds and compare their opinions. Their manners were somewhat coarse, but their conversation was instructive, and their disputations acute, though sometimes too violent and often continued till neither controvertist remembered upon what question they began. Some faults were almost general among them: everyone was desirous to dictate to the rest, and everyone was pleased to hear the genius or knowledge of another depreciated.

In this assembly Rasselas was relating his interview with the hermit and the wonder with which he heard him censure a course of life which he had so deliberately chosen and so laudably followed. The sentiments of the hearers were various. Some were of opinion that the folly of his choice had been justly punished by condemnation to perpetual perseverance. One of the youngest among them, with great vehemence, pronounced him a hypocrite. Some talked of the right of society to the labor of individuals, and considered retirement as a desertion of duty. Others readily allowed that there was a time when the claims of the public were satisfied and when a man might properly sequester himself, to review his life and purify his heart.

One, who appeared more affected with the narrative than the rest, thought it likely that the hermit would, in a few years, go back to his retreat, and, perhaps, if shame did not restrain or death intercept him, return once more from this retreat into the world: "For the hope of happiness," said he, "is so strongly impressed that the longest experience is not able to efface it. Of the present state, whatever it be, we feel and are forced to confess the misery; yet, when the same state is again at a distance, imagination paints it as desirable. But the time will surely come when desire will be no longer our torment, and no man shall be wretched but by his own fault."

"This," said a philosopher who had heard him with tokens of great impatience, "is the present condition of a wise man. The time is already come when none are wretched but by their own fault. Nothing is more idle than to inquire after happiness, which nature has kindly placed within our reach. The way to be happy is to live according to nature, in obedience to that universal and unalterable law with which every heart is originally impressed; which is not written on it by precept, but engraven by destiny; not instilled by education, but infused at our nativity. He that lives according to nature will suffer nothing from the delusions of hope or importunities of desire; he will receive and reject with equability of temper, and act or suffer as the reason of things shall alternately prescribe. Other men may amuse themselves with subtle definitions or intricate ratiocinations. Let them learn to be wise by easier means. Let them observe the hind of the forest and the linnet of the grove; let them consider the life of animals, whose motions are regulated by instinct; they obey their guide, and are happy. Let us therefore, at length, cease to dispute, and learn to live; throw away the encumbrance of precepts, which they who utter them with so much pride and pomp do not understand, and carry with us this simple and intelligible maxim — that deviation from nature is deviation from happiness."

When he had spoken, he looked round him with a placid air, and enjoyed the consciousness of his own beneficence. "Sir," said the prince with great modesty, "as I, like all the rest of mankind, am desirous of felicity, my closest attention has been fixed upon your discourse; I doubt not the truth of a position which a man so learned has so confidently advanced. Let me only know what it is to live according to nature."

"When I find young men so humble and so docile," said the philosopher, "I can deny them no information which my studies have enabled me to afford. To live according to nature is to act always with due regard to the fitness arising from the relations and qualities of causes and effects; to concur with the great and unchangeable scheme of universal felicity; to cooperate with the general disposition and tendency of the present system of things."

The prince soon found that this was one of the sages whom he should understand less as he heard him longer. He therefore bowed and was silent, and the philosopher, supposing him satisfied and the rest vanquished, rose up and departed with the air of a man that had cooperated with the present system.

The Prince and His Sister
Divide between Them the
Work of Observation

23 RASSELAS returned home full of reflections, doubtful how to direct his future steps. Of the way to happiness he found the learned and simple equally ignorant, but, as he was yet young, he flattered himself that he had time remaining for more experiments and further inquiries. He communicated to Imlac his observations and his doubts, but was answered by him with new doubts and remarks that gave him no comfort. He therefore discoursed more frequently and freely with his sister, who had yet the same hope with himself and always assisted him to give some reason why, though he had been hitherto frustrated, he might succeed at last.

"We have hitherto," said she, "known but little of the world. We have never yet been either great or mean. In our own country, though we had royalty, we had no power; and in this, we have not yet seen the private recesses of domestic peace. Imlac favors not our search, lest we should in time find him mistaken. We will divide the task between us. You shall try what is to be found in the splendor of courts, and I will range the shades of humbler life. Perhaps command and authority may be the supreme blessings, as they afford most opportunity of doing good; or, perhaps, what this world can give may be found in the modest habitations of middle fortune, too low for great designs and too high for penury and distress.''

The Prince Examines the Happiness of High Stations

24 RASSELAS applauded the design, and appeared next day with a splendid retinue at the court of the Bassa. He was soon distinguished for his magnificence, and admitted, as a prince whose curiosity had brought him from distant countries, to an intimacy with the great officers and frequent conversation with the Bassa himself.

He was at first inclined to believe that the man must be pleased with his own condition, whom all approached with reverence and heard with obedience, and who had the power to extend his edicts to a whole kingdom. "There can be no pleasure," said he, "equal to that of feeling at once the joy of thousands, all made happy by wise administration. Yet, since by the law of subordination this sublime delight can be in one nation but the lot of one, it is surely reasonable to think that there is some satisfaction more popular and accessible, and that millions can hardly be subjected to the will of a single man, only to fill his particular breast with incommunicable content."

These thoughts were often in his mind, and he found no solution of the difficulty. But, as presents and civilities gained him more familiarity, he found that almost every man who stood high in employment hated all the rest, and was hated by them, and that their lives were a continual succession of plots and detections, stratagems and escapes, faction and treachery. Many of those who surrounded the Bassa were sent only to watch and report his conduct; every tongue was muttering censure, and every eye was searching for a fault.

At last the letters of revocation arrived; the Bassa was carried in chains to Constantinople, and his name was mentioned no more.

"What are we now to think of the prerogatives of power?" said Rasselas to his sister. "Is it without any efficacy to good? Or is the subordinate degree only dangerous, and the supreme safe and glorious? Is the Sultan the only happy man in his dominions? Or is the Sultan himself subject to the torments of suspicion and the dread of enemies?"

In a short time the second Bassa was deposed; the Sultan that had advanced him was murdered by the Janizaries, and his successor had other views and different favorites.

The Princess Pursues Her Inquiry with More Diligence than Success

25 THE princess, in the mean time, insinuated herself into many families, for there are few doors through which liberality, joined with good humor, cannot find its way. The daughters of many houses were airy and cheerful, but Nekayah had been too long accustomed to the conversation of Imlac and her brother to be much pleased with childish levity and prattle which had no meaning. She found their thoughts narrow, their wishes low, and their merriment often artificial. Their pleasures, poor as they were, could not be preserved pure, but were embittered by petty competitions and worthless emulation. They were always jealous of the beauty of each other, of a quality to which solicitude can add nothing and from which detraction can take nothing away. Many were in love with triflers like themselves, and many fancied that they were in love when in truth they were only idle. Their affection was

not fixed on sense or virtue, and therefore seldom ended but in vexation. Their grief, however, like their joy, was transient; everything floated in their mind unconnected with the past or future, so that one desire easily gave way to another, as a second stone cast into the water effaces and confounds the circles of the first.

With these girls she played as with inoffensive animals, and found them proud of her countenance and weary of her company.

But her purpose was to examine more deeply, and her affability easily persuaded the hearts that were swelling with sorrow to discharge their secrets in her ear; and those whom hope flattered, or prosperity delighted, often courted her to partake their pleasures.

The princess and her brother commonly met in the evening, in a private summer house on the bank of the Nile, and related to each other the occurrences of the day. As they were sitting together, the princess cast her eyes upon the river that flowed before her. "Answer," said she, "great Father of Waters, thou that rollest thy floods through eighty nations, to the invocations of the daughter of thy native king. Tell me if thou waterest, through all thy course, a single habitation from which thou dost not hear the murmurs of complaint?"

"You are, then," said Rasselas, "not more successful in private houses than I have been in courts." "I have, since the last partition of our provinces," said the princess, "enabled myself to enter familiarly into many families, where there was the fairest show of prosperity and peace, and know not one house that is not haunted by some fury that destroys their quiet.

"I did not seek ease among the poor, because I concluded that there it could not be found. But I saw many poor whom I had supposed to live in affluence. Poverty has, in large cities, very different appearances; it is often concealed in splendor, and often in extravagance. It is the care of a very great part of mankind to conceal their indigence from the rest; they support themselves by temporary expedients, and every day is lost in contriving for the morrow.

"This, however, was an evil which, though frequent, I saw with less pain, because I could relieve it. Yet some have refused my bounties, more offended with my quickness to detect their wants than pleased with my readiness to succor them; and others, whose exigencies compelled them to admit my kindness, have never been able to forgive their benefactress. Many, however, have been sincerely grateful, without the ostentation of gratitude or hope of other favors."

The Princess Continues Her Remarks
upon Private Life

26 NEKAYAH, perceiving her brother's attention fixed, proceeded in her narrative.
"In families where there is not poverty, there is commonly discord. If a kingdom be, as Imlac tells us, a great family, a family likewise is a little kingdom, torn with factions and exposed to revolutions. An unpracticed observer expects the love of parents and children to be constant and equal, but this kindness seldom continues beyond the years of infancy. In a short time the children become rivals to their parents; benefits are allayed by reproaches, and gratitude debased by envy.

"Parents and children seldom act in concert. Each child endeavors to appropriate the esteem or fondness of the parents, and the parents, with yet less temptation, betray each other to their children; thus, some place their confidence in the father, and some in the mother, and by degrees the house is filled with artifices and feuds.

"The opinions of children and parents, of the young and the old, are naturally opposite, by the contrary effects of hope and despondence, of expectation and experience, without crime or folly on either side. The colors of life in youth and age appear different, as the face of nature in spring and winter. And how can children credit the assertions of parents, which their own eyes show them to be false?

"Few parents act in such a manner as much to enforce their maxims by the credit of their lives. The old man trusts wholly to slow contrivance and gradual progression; the youth expects to force his way by genius, vigor, and precipitance. The old man pays regard to riches, and the youth reverences virtue. The old man deifies prudence; the youth commits himself to magnanimity and chance. The young man, who intends no ill, believes that none is intended, and therefore acts with openness and candor; but his father, having suffered the injuries of fraud, is impelled to suspect and too often allured to practice it. Age looks with anger on the temerity of youth, and youth with contempt on the scrupulosity of age. Thus parents and children, for the greatest part, live on to love less and less; and, if those whom nature has thus closely united are the torments of each other, where shall we look for tenderness and consolation?"

"Surely," said the prince, "you must have been unfortunate in your choice of acquaintance. I am unwilling to believe that the most tender of all relations is thus impeded in its effects by natural necessity."

"Domestic discord," answered she, "is not inevitably and fatally necessary, but yet it is not easily avoided. We seldom see that a whole family is virtuous; the good and evil cannot well agree; and the evil can yet less agree with one another; even the virtuous fall sometimes to variance, when their virtues are of different kinds and tending to extremes. In general, those parents have most reverence who most deserve it, for he that lives well cannot be despised.

"Many other evils infest private life. Some are the slaves of servants whom they have trusted with their affairs. Some are kept in continual anxiety by the caprice of rich relations, whom they cannot please, and dare not offend. Some husbands are imperious, and some wives perverse; and, as it is always more easy to do evil than good, though the wisdom or virtue of one can very rarely make many happy, the folly or vice of one may often make many miserable."

"If such be the general effect of marriage," said the prince, "I shall, for the future, think it dangerous to connect my interest with that of another, lest I should be unhappy by my partner's fault."

"I have met," said the princess, "with many who live single for that reason, but I never found their prudence ought to raise envy. They dream away their time without friendship, without fondness, and are driven to rid themselves of the day, for which they have no use, by childish amusements or vicious delights. They act as beings under the constant sense of some known inferiority that fills their minds with rancor and their tongues with censure. They are peevish at home and malevolent abroad, and, as the outlaws of human nature, make it their business and their pleasure to disturb that society which debars them from its privileges. To live without feeling or exciting sympathy, to be fortunate without adding to the felicity of others, or afflicted without tasting the balm of pity, is a state more gloomy than solitude. It is not retreat, but exclusion from mankind. Marriage has many pains, but celibacy has no pleasures."

"What then is to be done?" said Rasselas. "The more we inquire, the less we can resolve. Surely he is most likely to please himself that has no other inclination to regard."

Disquisition upon Greatness

27 ⟨image⟩ THE conversation had a short pause. The prince, having considered his sister's observations, told her that she had surveyed life with prejudice, and supposed misery where she did not find it. "Your narrative," says he, "throws yet a darker gloom upon the prospects of futurity; the predictions of Imlac were but faint sketches of the evils painted by Nekayah. I have been lately convinced that quiet is not the daughter of grandeur or of power, that her presence is not to be bought by wealth, nor enforced by conquest. It is evident that, as any man acts in a wider compass, he must be more exposed to opposition from enmity or miscarriage from chance. Whoever has many to please or to govern must use the ministry of many agents, some of whom will be wicked and some ignorant; by some he will be misled, and by others betrayed. If he gratifies one, he will offend another; those that are not favored will think themselves injured; and, since favors can be conferred but upon few, the greater number will be always discontented."

"The discontent," said the princess, "which is thus unreasonable, I hope that I shall always have spirit to despise, and you power to repress."

"Discontent," answered Rasselas, "will not always be without reason, under the most just and vigilant administration of public affairs. None, however attentive, can always discover that merit which indigence or faction may happen to obscure; and none, however powerful, can always reward it. Yet he that sees inferior desert advanced above him will naturally impute that preference to partiality or caprice; and, indeed, it can scarcely be hoped that any man, however magnanimous by nature or exalted by condition, will be able to persist forever in the fixed and inexorable justice of distribution. He will sometimes indulge his own affections, and sometimes those of his favorites; he will permit some to please him who can never serve him; he will discover in those whom he loves qualities which, in reality, they do not possess; and to those from whom he receives pleasure, he will in his turn endeavor to give it. Thus will recommendations sometimes prevail which were purchased by money or by more destructive bribery of flattery and servility.

"He that has much to do will do something wrong, and of that wrong must suffer the consequences; and, if it were possible that he should always act rightly, yet when such numbers are to judge of his conduct, the bad will censure and obstruct him by malevolence, and the good sometimes by mistake.

"The highest stations cannot therefore hope to

be abodes of happiness, which I would willingly believe to have fled from thrones and palaces to seats of humble privacy and placid obscurity. For what can hinder the satisfaction or intercept the expectations of him whose abilities are adequate to his employments, who sees with his own eyes the whole circuit of his influence, who chooses by his own knowledge all whom he trusts, and whom none are tempted to deceive by hope or fear? Surely he has nothing to do but to love and to be loved, to be virtuous and to be happy."

"Whether perfect happiness would be procured by perfect goodness," said Nekayah, "this world will never afford an opportunity of deciding. But this, at least, may be maintained: that we do not always find visible happiness in proportion to visible virtue. All natural and almost all political evils are incident alike to the bad and good; they are confounded in the misery of a famine and not much distinguished in the fury of a faction; they sink together in a tempest, and are driven together from their country by invaders. All that virtue can afford is quietness of conscience and a steady prospect of a happier state; this may enable us to endure calamity with patience, but remember that patience must suppose pain."

Rasselas and Nekayah Continue Their Conversation

28 "DEAR princess," said Rasselas, "you fall into the common errors of exaggeratory declamation, by producing, in a familiar disquisition, examples of national calamities and scenes of extensive misery, which are found in books rather than in the world and which, as they are horrid, are ordained to be rare. Let us not imagine evils which we do not feel, nor injure life by misrepresentations. I cannot bear that querulous eloquence which threatens every city with a siege like that of Jerusalem, that makes famine attend on every flight of locusts and suspends pestilence on the wing of every blast that issues from the south.

"On necessary and inevitable evils which overwhelm kingdoms at once, all disputation is vain; when they happen, they must be endured. But it is evident that these bursts of universal distress are more dreaded than felt; thousands and ten thousands flourish in youth and wither in age, without the knowledge of any other than domestic evils, and share the same pleasures and vexations, whether their kings are mild or cruel, whether the armies of their country pursue their enemies or retreat before them. While courts are disturbed with intestine competitions and ambassadors are negotiating in foreign countries, the smith still plies his anvil, and the husbandman drives his plough forward; the necessaries of life are required and obtained, and the successive business of the seasons continues to make its wonted revolutions.

"Let us cease to consider, what perhaps may never happen, and what, when it shall happen, will laugh at human speculation. We will not endeavor to modify the motions of the elements, or to fix the destiny of kingdoms. It is our business to consider what beings like us may perform, each laboring for his own happiness, by promoting within his circle, however narrow, the happiness of others.

"Marriage is evidently the dictate of nature; men and women are made to be companions of each other; and therefore I cannot be persuaded but that marriage is one of the means of happiness."

"I know not," said the princess, "whether marriage be more than one of the innumerable modes of human misery. When I see and reckon the various forms of connubial infelicity, the unexpected causes of lasting discord, the diversities of temper, the oppositions of opinion, the rude collisions of contrary desire where both are urged by violent impulses, the obstinate contests of disagreeing virtues where both are supported by consciousness of good intention, I am sometimes disposed to think with the severer casuists of most nations that marriage is rather permitted than approved, and that none, but by the instigation of a passion too much indulged, entangle themselves with indissoluble compacts."

"You seem to forget," replied Rasselas, "that you have, even now, represented celibacy as less happy than marriage. Both conditions may be bad, but they cannot both be worst. Thus it happens when wrong opinions are entertained, that they mutually destroy each other, and leave the mind open to truth."

"I did not expect," answered the princess, "to hear that imputed to falsehood which is the consequence only of frailty. To the mind, as to the eye, it is difficult to compare with exactness objects vast in their extent and various in their parts. Where we see or conceive the whole at once, we readily note the discriminations and decide the preference; but of two systems, of which neither can be surveyed by any human being in its full compass of magnitude and multiplicity of complecation, where is the wonder that, judging of the whole by parts, I am alternately affected by one and the other, as either presses on my memory or fancy? We differ from ourselves, just as we differ from each other, when we see only part of the question, as in the multifarious relations of politics and morality; but, when we perceive the whole at once, as in numerical computations, all agree in one judgment, and none ever varies his opinion."

"Let us not add," said the prince, "to the other evils of life the bitterness of controversy, nor endeavor to vie with each other in subtilities of argument. We are employed in a search, of which both are equally to enjoy the success, or suffer by the miscarriage. It is therefore fit that we assist each other. You surely conclude too hastily from the infelicity of marriage against its institution. Will not the misery of life prove equally that life cannot be the gift of heaven? The world must be peopled by marriage, or peopled without it."

"How the world is to be peopled," returned Nekayah, "is not my care, and needs not be yours. I see no danger that the present generation should omit to leave successors behind them. We are not now inquiring for the world, but for ourselves."

The Debate of Marriage Continued

29 "THE good of the whole," says Rasselas, "is the same with the good of all its parts. If marriage be best for mankind, it must be evidently best for individuals; or a permanent and necessary duty must be the cause of evil, and some must be inevitably sacrificed to the convenience of others. In the estimate which you have made of the two states, it appears that the incommodities of a single life are, in a great measure, necessary and certain, but those of the conjugal state accidental and avoidable.

"I cannot forbear to flatter myself that prudence and benevolence will make marriage happy. The general folly of mankind is the cause of general complaint. What can be expected but disappointment and repentance from a choice made in the immaturity of youth, in the ardor of desire, without judgment, without foresight, without inquiry after conformity of opinions, similarity of manners, rectitude of judgment, or purity of sentiment?

"Such is the common process of marriage. A

youth and maiden, meeting by chance or brought together by artifice, exchange glances, reciprocate civilities, go home, and dream of one another. Having little to divert attention or diversify thought, they find themselves uneasy when they are apart, and therefore conclude that they shall be happy together. They marry, and discover what nothing but voluntary blindness before had concealed; they wear out life in altercations, and charge nature with cruelty.

"From those early marriages proceeds likewise the rivalry of parents and children. The son is eager to enjoy the world before the father is willing to forsake it, and there is hardly room at once for two generations. The daughter begins to bloom before the mother can be content to fade, and neither can forbear to wish for the absence of the other.

"Surely all these evils may be avoided by that deliberation and delay which prudence prescribes to irrevocable choice. In the variety and jollity of youthful pleasures, life may be well enough supported without the help of a partner. Longer time will increase experience, and wider views will allow better opportunities of inquiry and selection. One advantage, at least, will be certain: the parents will be visibly older than their children."

"What reason cannot collect," said Nekayah, "and what experiment has not yet taught can be known only from the report of others. I have been told that late marriages are not eminently happy. This is a question too important to be neglected, and I have often proposed it to those whose accuracy of remark and comprehensiveness of knowledge made their suffrages worthy of regard. They have generally determined that it is dangerous for a man and woman to suspend their fate upon each other at a time when opinions are fixed, and habits are established; when friendships have been contracted on both sides; when life has been planned into method, and the mind has long enjoyed the contemplation of its own prospects.

"It is scarcely possible that two travelling through the world under the conduct of chance should have been both directed to the same path, and it will not often happen that either will quit the track which custom has made pleasing. When the desultory levity of youth has settled into regularity, it is soon succeeded by pride ashamed to yield, or obstinacy delighting to contend. And, even though mutual esteem produces mutual desire to please, time itself, as it modifies unchangeably the external mien, determines likewise the direction of the passions, and gives an inflexible rigidity to the manners. Long customs are not easily broken. He that attempts to change the course of his own life very often labors in vain, and how shall we do that for others which we are seldom able to do for ourselves?"

"But surely," interposed the prince, "you suppose the chief motive of choice forgotten or neglected. Whenever I shall seek a wife, it shall be my first question, whether she be willing to be led by reason."

"Thus it is," said Nekayah, "that philosophers are deceived. There are a thousand familiar disputes which reason never can decide; questions that elude investigation, and make logic ridiculous; cases where something must be done, and where little can be said. Consider the state of mankind, and inquire how few can be supposed to act upon any occasions, whether small or great, with all the reasons of action present to their minds. Wretched would be the pair above all names of wretchedness, who should be doomed to adjust by reason, every morning, all the minute detail of a domestic day.

"Those who marry at an advanced age will probably escape the encroachments of their children; but, in diminution of this advantage, they will be likely to leave them, ignorant and helpless, to a guardian's mercy; or, if that should not happen, they must at least go out of the world before they see those whom they love best either wise or great.

"From their children, if they have less to fear, they have less also to hope, and they lose, without equivalent, the joys of early love and the convenience of uniting with manners pliant and minds susceptible of new impressions, which might wear away their dissimilitudes by long cohabitation, as soft bodies, by continual attrition, conform their surfaces to each other.

"I believe it will be found that those who marry late are best pleased with their children, and those who marry early, with their partners."

"The union of these two affections," said Rasselas, "would produce all that could be wished. Perhaps there is a time when marriage might unite them, a time neither too early for the father nor too late for the husband."

"Every hour," answered the princess, "confirms my prejudice in favor of the position so often uttered by the mouth of Imlac: that nature sets her gifts on the right hand and on the left. Those conditions which flatter hope and attract desire are so constituted that, as we approach one, we recede from another. There are goods so opposed that we cannot seize both, but, by too much prudence, may pass between them at too great a distance to reach either. This is often the fate of long consideration. He does nothing who endeavors to do more than is allowed to humanity. Flatter not yourself with contrarieties of pleasure. Of the blessings set before you, make your choice, and be content. No man can taste the fruits of autumn while he is delighting his scent with the flowers of the spring; no man can, at the same time, fill his cup from the source and from the mouth of the Nile."

Imlac Enters and Changes the Conversation

30 HERE Imlac entered and interrupted them. "Imlac," said Rasselas, "I have been taking from the princess the dismal history of private life, and am almost discouraged from further search."

"It seems to me," said Imlac, "that while you are making the choice of life, you neglect to live. You wander about a single city, which, however large and diversified, can now afford few novelties, and forget that you are in a country famous among the earliest monarchies for the power and wisdom of its inhabitants; a country where the sciences first dawned that illuminate the world, and beyond which the arts cannot be traced of civil society or domestic life.

"The old Egyptians have left behind them monuments of industry and power, before which all European magnificence is confessed to fade away. The ruins of their architecture are the schools of

modern builders, and, from the wonders which
time has spared, we may conjecture, though un-
certainly, what it has destroyed."

"My curiosity," said Rasselas, "does not very
strongly lead me to survey piles of stone, or mounds
of earth. My business is with man. I came hither
not to measure fragments of temples or trace choked
aqueducts, but to look upon the various scenes of
the present world."

"The things that are now before us," said the
princess, "require attention and deserve it. What
have I to do with the heroes or the monuments of
ancient times? With times which never can return
and heroes whose form of life was different from
all that the present condition of mankind requires
or allows?"

"To know anything," returned the poet, "we
must know its effects; to see men we must see their
works, that we may learn what reason has dictated
or passion has incited, and find what are the most
powerful motives of action. To judge rightly of the
present, we must oppose it to the past, for all
judgment is comparative, and of the future nothing
can be known. The truth is that no mind is much
employed upon the present; recollection and anticipation fill up almost all our moments. Our passions
are joy and grief, love and hatred, hope and fear.
Of joy and grief the past is the object, and the
future of hope and fear. Even love and hatred
respect the past, for the cause must have been before the effect.

"The present state of things is the consequence
of the former, and it is natural to inquire what

were the sources of the good that we enjoy or the evil that we suffer. If we act only for ourselves, to neglect the study of history is not prudent; if we are entrusted with the care of others, it is not just. Ignorance, when it is voluntary, is criminal; and he may properly be charged with evil who refused to learn how he might prevent it.

"There is no part of history so generally useful as that which relates the progress of the human mind, the gradual improvement of reason, the successive advances of science, the vicissitudes of learning and ignorance, which are the light and darkness of thinking beings, the extinction and resuscitation of arts, and the revolutions of the intellectual world. If accounts of battles and invasions are peculiarly the business of princes, the useful or elegant arts are not to be neglected; those who have kingdoms to govern have understandings to cultivate.

"Example is always more efficacious than precept. A soldier is formed in war, and a painter must copy pictures. In this, contemplative life has the advantage — great actions are seldom seen, but the labors of art are always at hand for those who desire to know what art has been able to perform.

"When the eye or the imagination is struck with an uncommon work, the next transition of an active mind is to the means by which it was performed. Here begins the true use of such contemplation; we enlarge our comprehension by new ideas and perhaps recover some art lost to mankind, or learn what is less perfectly known in our own country.

At least we compare our own with former times, and either rejoice at our improvements, or, what is the first motion towards good, discover our defects."

"I am willing," said the prince, "to see all that can deserve my search." "And I," said the princess, "shall rejoice to learn something of the manners of antiquity."

"The most pompous monument of Egyptian greatness and one of the most bulky works of manual industry," said Imlac, "are the Pyramids, fabrics raised before the time of history and of which the earliest narratives afford us only uncertain traditions. Of these the greatest is still standing, very little injured by time."

"Let us visit them tomorrow," said Nekayah. "I have often heard of the Pyramids, and shall not rest till I have seen them, within and without, with my own eyes."

They Visit the Pyramids

31 ❦ THE resolution being thus taken, they set out the next day. They laid tents upon their camels, being resolved to stay among the Pyramids till their curiosity was fully satisfied. They travelled gently, turned aside to everything remarkable, stopped from time to time and conversed with the inhabitants, and observed the various appearances of towns ruined and inhabited, of wild and cultivated nature.

When they came to the great Pyramid, they were astonished at the extent of the base and the height of the top. Imlac explained to them the principles upon which the pyramidal form was chosen for a fabric intended to co-extend its duration with that of the world. He showed that its gradual diminution gave it such stability as defeated all the common attacks of the elements, and could scarcely be overthrown by earthquakes themselves, the least resistible of natural violence. A concussion that should shatter the Pyramid would threaten the dissolution of the continent.

They measured all its dimensions, and pitched their tents at its foot. Next day they prepared to enter its interior apartments and, having hired the common guides, climbed up to the first passage, when the favorite of the princess, looking into the cavity, stepped back and trembled. "Pekuah," said the princess, "of what art thou afraid?" "Of the narrow entrance," answered the lady, "and of the dreadful gloom. I dare not enter a place which must surely be inhabited by unquiet souls. The original possessors of these dreadful vaults will start up before us and perhaps shut us in forever." She spoke and threw her arms round the neck of her mistress.

"If all your fear be of apparitions," said the prince, "I will promise you safety. There is no danger from the dead. He that is once buried will be seen no more."

"That the dead are seen no more," said Imlac, "I will not undertake to maintain, against the concurrent and unvaried testimony of all ages and of all nations. There is no people, rude or learned, among whom apparitions of the dead are not re-lated and believed. This opinion, which perhaps prevails as far as human nature is diffused, could become universal only by its truth. Those that never heard of one another would not have agreed in a tale which nothing but experience can make credible. That it is doubted by single cavillers can very little weaken the general evidence, and some who deny it with their tongues confess it by their fears.

"Yet I do not mean to add new terrors to those

which have already seized upon Pekuah. There can be no reason why spectres should haunt the Pyramid more than other places, or why they should have power or will to hurt innocence and purity. Our entrance is no violation of their privileges. We can take nothing from them. How then can we offend them?"

"My dear Pekuah," said the princess, "I will always go before you, and Imlac shall follow you. Remember that you are the companion of the princess of Abyssinia."

"If the princess is pleased that her servant should die," returned the lady, "let her command some death less dreadful than enclosure in this horrid cavern. You know I dare not disobey you. I must go if you command me, but, if I once enter, I never shall come back."

The princess saw that her fear was too strong for expostulation or reproof, and, embracing her, told her that she should stay in the tent till their return. Pekuah was yet not satisfied, but entreated the princess not to pursue so dreadful a purpose as that of entering the recesses of the Pyramid. "Though I cannot teach courage," said Nekayah, "I must not learn cowardice, nor leave at last undone what I came hither only to do."

They Enter the Pyramid

32   PEKUAH descended to the tents, and the rest entered the Pyramid. They passed through the galleries, surveyed the vaults of marble, and examined the chest in which the body of the founder is supposed to have been reposited. They then sat down in one of the most spacious chambers to rest a while before they attempted to return.

"We have now," said Imlac, "gratified our minds with an exact view of the greatest work of man, except the wall of China.

"Of the wall it is very easy to assign the motive. It secured a wealthy and timorous nation from the incursion of barbarians, whose unskilfulness in arts made it easier for them to supply their wants by rapine than by industry, and who from time to time poured in upon the habitations of peaceful commerce, as vultures descend upon domestic fowl. Their celerity and fierceness made the wall necessary, and their ignorance made it efficacious.

"But for the Pyramids no reason has ever been

given adequate to the cost and labor of the work. The narrowness of the chambers proves that it could afford no retreat from enemies, and treasures might have been reposited at far less expense with equal security. It seems to have been erected only in compliance with that hunger of imagination which preys incessantly upon life, and must be always appeased by some employment. Those who have already all that they can enjoy must enlarge their desires. He that has built for use, till use is supplied, must begin to build for vanity, and extend his plan to the utmost power of human performance, that he may not be soon reduced to form another wish.

"I consider this mighty structure as a monument of the insufficiency of human enjoyments. A king whose power is unlimited, and whose treasures surmount all real and imaginary wants, is compelled to solace, by the erection of a Pyramid, the satiety of dominion and tastelessness of pleasures, and to amuse the tediousness of declining life, by seeing thousands laboring without end, and one stone, for no purpose, laid upon another. Whoever thou art that, not content with a moderate condition, imaginest happiness in royal magnificence and dreamest that command or riches can feed the appetite of novelty with perpetual gratifications, survey the Pyramids, and confess thy folly!"

The Princess Meets with an Unexpected Misfortune

33 THEY rose up, and returned through the cavity at which they had entered, and the princess prepared for her favorite a long narrative of dark labyrinths and costly rooms, and of the different impressions which the varieties of the way had made upon her. But when they came to their train, they found everyone silent and dejected; the men discovered shame and fear in their countenances, and the women were weeping in the tents.

What had happened they did not try to conjecture, but immediately inquired. "You had scarcely entered into the Pyramid," said one of the attendants, "when a troop of Arabs rushed upon us; we were too few to resist them and too slow to escape. They were about to search the tents, set us on our camels, and drive us along before them, when the approach of some Turkish horsemen put them to flight; but they seized the lady Pekuah with her two maids, and carried them away. The Turks are now pursuing them by our instigation, but I fear they will not be able to overtake them."

The princess was overpowered with surprise and grief. Rasselas, in the first heat of his resentment, ordered his servants to follow him and prepared to pursue the robbers with his sabre in his hand. "Sir," said Imlac, "what can you hope from violence or valor? The Arabs are mounted on horses trained to battle and retreat; we have only beasts of burden. By leaving our present station, we may lose the princess, but cannot hope to regain Pekuah."

In a short time the Turks returned, having not been able to reach the enemy. The princess burst out into new lamentations, and Rasselas could scarcely forbear to reproach them with cowardice; but Imlac was of opinion that the escape of the Arabs was no addition to their misfortune, for perhaps they would have killed their captives rather than have resigned them.

They Return to Cairo without Pekuah

34 THERE was nothing to be hoped from longer stay. They returned to Cairo, repenting of their curiosity, censuring the negligence of the government, lamenting their own rashness which had neglected to procure a guard, imagining many expedients by which the loss of Pekuah might have been prevented, and resolving to do something for her recovery, though none could find anything proper to be done.

Nekayah retired to her chamber, where her women attempted to comfort her by telling her that all had their troubles and that lady Pekuah had enjoyed much happiness in the world for a long time and might reasonably expect a change of fortune. They hoped that some good would befall her wheresoever she was and that their mistress would find another friend who might supply her place.

The princess made them no answer, and they continued the form of condolence, not much grieved in their hearts that the favorite was lost.

Next day the prince presented to the Bassa a memorial of the wrong which he had suffered, and a petition for redress. The Bassa threatened to punish the robbers, but did not attempt to catch them; nor indeed could any account or description be given by which he might direct the pursuit.

It soon appeared that nothing would be done by authority. Governors, being accustomed to hear of more crimes than they can punish and more wrongs than they can redress, set themselves at ease by indiscriminate negligence, and presently forget the request when they lose sight of the petitioner.

Imlac then endeavored to gain some intelligence by private agents. He found many who pretended to an exact knowledge of all the haunts of the Arabs and to regular correspondence with their chiefs, and who readily undertook the recovery of Pekuah. Of these, some were furnished with money for their journey, and came back no more; some were liberally paid for accounts which a few days discovered to be false. But the princess would not suffer any means, however improbable, to be left untried. While she was doing something, she kept her hope alive. As one expedient failed, another was suggested; when one messenger returned unsuccessful, another was dispatched to a different quarter.

Two months had now passed, and of Pekuah nothing had been heard; the hopes which they had endeavored to raise in each other grew more languid, and the princess, when she saw nothing more to be tried, sunk down inconsolable in hopeless dejection. A thousand times she reproached herself with the easy compliance by which she permitted her favorite to stay behind her. "Had not my fondness," said she, "lessened my authority, Pekuah had not dared to talk of her terrors. She ought to have feared me more than spectres. A severe look would have overpowered her; a peremptory command would have compelled obedience. Why did foolish indulgence prevail upon me? Why did I not speak, and refuse to hear?"

"Great princess," said Imlac, "do not reproach yourself for your virtue, or consider that as blamable by which evil has accidentally been caused. Your tenderness for the timidity of Pekuah was generous and kind. When we act according to our duty, we commit the event to him by whose laws our actions are governed and who will suffer none to be finally punished for obedience. When, in prospect of some good, whether natural or moral, we break the rules prescribed us, we withdraw from the direction of superior wisdom, and take all consequences upon ourselves. Man cannot so far know the connection of causes and events as that he may venture to do wrong in order to do right. When we pursue our end by lawful means, we may always console our miscarriage by the hope of future recompense. When we consult only our own policy and attempt to find a nearer way to good, by overleaping the settled boundaries of right and wrong, we cannot be happy even by success, because we cannot escape the consciousness of our fault; but, if we miscarry, the disappointment is irremediably embittered. How comfortless is the sorrow of him who feels at once the pangs of guilt and the vexation of calamity, which guilt has brought upon him!

"Consider, princess, what would have been your condition, if the lady Pekuah had entreated to accompany you, and, being compelled to stay in the tents, had been carried away? Or how would you have borne the thought if you had forced her into the Pyramid and she had died before you in agonies of terror?"

"Had either happened," said Nekayah, "I could not have endured life till now. I should have been tortured to madness by the remembrance of such cruelty, or must have pined away in abhorrence of myself."

"This at least," said Imlac, "is the present reward of virtuous conduct, that no unlucky consequence can oblige us to repent it."

The Princess Languishes for Want of Pekuah

35   NEKAYAH, being thus reconciled to herself, found that no evil is insupportable, but that which is accompanied with consciousness of wrong. She was from that time delivered from the violence of tempestuous sorrow and sunk into silent pensiveness and gloomy tranquillity. She sat from morning to evening, recollecting all that had been done or said by her Pekuah, treasured up with care every trifle on which Pekuah had set an accidental value and which might recall to mind any little incident or careless conversation. The sentiments of her whom she now expected to see no more were treasured in her memory as rules of life, and she deliberated to no other end than to conjecture, on any occasion, what would have been the opinion and counsel of Pekuah.

The women by whom she was attended knew nothing of her real condition, and therefore she could not talk to them but with caution and reserve. She began to remit her curiosity, having no great care to collect notions which she had no convenience of uttering. Rasselas endeavored first to comfort, and afterward to divert her; he hired musicians, to whom she seemed to listen, but did hear them; and procured masters to instruct her in various arts, whose lectures, when they visited her again, were again to be repeated. She had lost her taste of pleasure and her ambition of excellence. And her mind, though forced into short excursions, always recurred to the image of her friend.

Imlac was every morning earnestly enjoined to renew his inquiries, and was asked every night whether he had yet heard of Pekuah, till, not being able to return the princess the answer that she desired, he was less and less willing to come into her presence. She observed his backwardness, and commanded him to attend her. "You are not," said she, "to confound impatience with resentment, or to suppose that I charge you with negligence, because I repine at your unsuccessfulness. I do not much wonder at your absence; I know that the unhappy are never pleasing and that all naturally avoid the contagion of misery. To hear complaints is wearisome alike to the wretched and the happy; for who would cloud, by adventitious grief, the short gleams of gaiety which life allows us? Or who that is struggling under his own evils will add to them the miseries of another?

"The time is at hand when none shall be disturbed any longer by the sighs of Nekayah; my search after happiness is now at an end. I am resolved to retire from the world with all its flatteries and deceits, and will hide myself in solitude, without any other care than to compose my thoughts and regulate my hours by a constant succession of innocent occupations, till, with a mind purified from all earthly desires, I shall enter into that state to which all are hastening and in which I hope again to enjoy the friendship of Pekuah."

"Do not entangle your mind," said Imlac, "by irrevocable determinations, nor increase the burden of life by a voluntary accumulation of misery. The weariness of retirement will continue or increase when the loss of Pekuah is forgotten. That you have been deprived of one pleasure is no very good reason for rejection of the rest."

"Since Pekuah was taken from me," said the princess, "I have no pleasure to reject or to retain. She that has no one to love or trust has little to hope. She wants the radical principle of happiness. We may, perhaps, allow that what satisfaction this world can afford must arise from the conjunction of wealth, knowledge, and goodness. Wealth is nothing but as it is bestowed, and knowledge nothing but as it is communicated; they must therefore be imparted to others, and to whom could I now delight to impart them? Goodness affords the only comfort which can be enjoyed without a partner, and goodness may be practiced in retirement."

"How far solitude may admit goodness or advance it, I shall not," replied Imlac, "dispute at present. Remember the confession of the pious hermit. You will wish to return into the world when the image of your companion has left your thoughts." "That time," said Nekayah, "will never come. The generous frankness, the modest obsequiousness, and the faithful secrecy of my dear Pekuah will always be more missed, as I shall live longer to see vice and folly."

"The state of a mind oppressed with a sudden calamity," said Imlac, "is like that of the fabulous inhabitants of the new-created earth, who, when the first night came upon them, supposed that day would never return. When the clouds of sorrow gather over us, we see nothing beyond them, nor can imagine how they will be dispelled; yet a new day succeeded to the night, and sorrow is never long without a dawn of ease. But they who restrain themselves from receiving comfort do as the savages would have done, had they put out their eyes when it was dark. Our minds, like our bodies, are in continual flux; something is hourly lost, and something acquired. To lose much at once is inconvenient to either, but, while the vital powers remain uninjured, nature will find the means of reparation. Distance has the same effect on the mind as on the eye, and, while we glide along the stream of time, whatever we leave behind us is always lessening, and that which we approach increasing, in magnitude. Do not suffer life to stagnate; it will grow muddy for want of motion. Commit yourself again to the current of the world; Pekuah will vanish by degrees. You will meet in your way some other favorite, or learn to diffuse yourself in general conversation."

"At least," said the prince, "do not despair before all remedies have been tried; the inquiry after the unfortunate lady is still continued, and shall be

carried on with yet greater diligence, on condition
that you will promise to wait a year for the event,
without any unalterable resolution.''

Nekayah thought this a reasonable demand, and
made the promise to her brother, who had been
advised by Imlac to require it. Imlac had, indeed,
no great hope of regaining Pekuah; but he supposed
that, if he could secure the interval of a year, the
princess would be then in no danger of a cloister.

Pekuah Is Still Remembered.
The Progress of Sorrow

36   NEKAYAH, seeing that nothing was omitted for the recovery of her favorite and having, by her promise, set her intention of retirement at a distance, began imperceptibly to return to common cares and common pleasures. She rejoiced without her own consent at the suspension of her sorrows, and sometimes caught herself with indignation in the act of turning away her mind from the remembrance of her whom yet she resolved never to forget.

She then appointed a certain hour of the day for meditation on the merits and fondness of Pekuah, and for some weeks retired constantly at the time fixed, and returned with her eyes swollen and her countenance clouded. By degrees she grew less scrupulous, and suffered any important and pressing avocation to delay the tribute of daily tears. She then yielded to less occasions, sometimes forgot what she was indeed afraid to remember, and at last wholly released herself from the duty of periodical affliction.

Her real love of Pekuah was yet not diminished. A thousand occurrences brought her back to memory, and a thousand wants, which nothing but the confidence of friendship can supply, made her frequently regretted. She therefore solicited Imlac never to desist from inquiry and to leave no art of intelligence untried, that at least she might have the comfort of knowing that she did not suffer by negligence or sluggishness. "Yet what," said she, "is to be expected from our pursuit of happiness, when we find the state of life to be such that happiness itself is the cause of misery? Why should we endeavor to attain that of which the possession cannot be secured? I shall henceforward fear to yield my heart to excellence, however bright, or to fondness, however tender, lest I should lose again what I have lost in Pekuah."

The Princess Hears News of Pekuah

37   IN seven months, one of the messengers, who had been sent away upon the day when the promise was drawn from the princess, returned, after many unsuccessful rambles, from the borders of Nubia, with an account that Pekuah was in the hands of an Arab chief who possessed a castle or fortress on the extremity of Egypt. The Arab, whose revenue was plunder, was willing to restore her, with her two attendants, for two hundred ounces of gold.

The price was no subject of debate. The princess was in ecstasies, when she heard that her favorite was alive, and might so cheaply be ransomed. She could not think of delaying for a moment Pekuah's happiness or her own, but entreated her brother to send back the messenger with the sum required. Imlac, being consulted, was not very confident of the veracity of the relator, and was still more doubtful of the Arab's faith, who might, if he were too liberally trusted, detain at once the money and the captives. He thought it dangerous to put themselves in the power of the Arab, by going into his district, and could not expect that the rover would so much expose himself as to come into the lower country, where he might be seized by the forces of the Bassa.

It is difficult to negotiate where neither will trust. But Imlac, after some deliberation, directed the messenger to propose that Pekuah should be conducted by ten horsemen to the monastery of St. Anthony, which is situated in the deserts of upper Egypt, where she should be met by the same number, and her ransom should be paid.

That no time might be lost, as they expected that the proposal would not be refused, they immediately began their journey to the monastery; and, when they arrived, Imlac went forward with the former messenger to the Arab's fortress. Rasselas was desirous to go with them, but neither his sister nor Imlac would consent. The Arab, according to the custom of his nation, observed the laws of hospitality with great exactness to those who put themselves into his power, and, in a few days, brought Pekuah with her maids, by easy journeys, to the place appointed, where, receiving the stipulated price, he restored her with great respect to liberty and her friends, and undertook to conduct them back towards Cairo, beyond all danger of robbery or violence.

The princess and her favorite embraced each other with transport too violent to be expressed, and went out together to pour the tears of tenderness in secret, and exchange professions of kindness and gratitude. After a few hours, they returned into the refectory of the convent where, in the presence of the prior and his brethren, the prince required of Pekuah the history of her adventures.

The Adventures of the Lady Pekuah

38 "AT what time and in what manner I was forced away," said Pekuah, "your servants have told you. The suddenness of the event struck me with surprise, and I was at first rather stupefied than agitated with any passion of either fear or sorrow. My confusion was increased by the speed and tumult of our flight, while we were followed by the Turks, who, as it seemed, soon despaired to overtake us, or were afraid of those whom they made a show of menacing.

"When the Arabs saw themselves out of danger, they slackened their course, and, as I was less harassed by external violence, I began to feel more uneasiness in my mind. After some time, we stopped near a spring shaded with trees in a pleasant meadow, where we were set upon the ground, and offered such refreshments as our masters were partaking. I was suffered to sit with my maids apart from the rest, and none attempted to comfort or insult us. Here I first began to feel the full weight of my misery. The girls sat weeping in silence, and from time to time looked on me for succor. I knew not to what condition we were doomed, nor could conjecture where would be the place of our captivity, or whence to draw any hope of deliverance. I was in the hands of robbers and savages, and had no reason to suppose that their pity was more than their justice, or that they would forbear the gratification of any ardor of desire or caprice of cruelty. I, however, kissed my maids, and endeavored to pacify them by remarking that we were yet treated with decency and that, since we were now carried beyond pursuit, there was no danger of violence to our lives.

"When we were to be set again on horseback, my maids clung round me, and refused to be parted; but I commanded them not to irritate those who had us in their power. We travelled the remaining part of the day through an unfrequented and pathless country, and came by moonlight to the side of a hill, where the rest of the troop were stationed. Their tents were pitched and their fires kindled, and our chief was welcomed as a man much beloved by his dependents.

"We were received into a large tent, where we found women who had attended their husbands in the expedition. They set before us the supper which they had provided, and I ate it rather to encourage my maids than to comply with any appetite of my own. When the meat was taken away, they spread the carpets for repose. I was weary, and hoped to find in sleep that remission of distress which nature seldom denies. Ordering myself therefore to be undressed, I observed that the women looked very earnestly upon me, not expecting, I suppose, to see me so submissively attended. When my upper vest was taken off, they were apparently struck with the splendor of my clothes, and one of them timorously laid her hand upon the embroidery. She then went out and in a short time came back with another woman, who seemed to be of higher rank and greater authority. She did, at her entrance, the usual act of reverence and, taking me by the hand, placed me in a smaller tent spread with finer carpets, where I spent the night quietly with my maids.

"In the morning, as I was sitting on the grass, the chief of the troop came towards me. I rose up to receive him, and he bowed with great respect. 'Illustrious lady,' said he, 'my fortune is better than I had presumed to hope. I am told by my women that I have a princess in my camp.' 'Sir,' answered I, 'your women have deceived themselves and you; I am not a princess, but an unhappy stranger, who intended soon to have left this country, in which I am now to be imprisoned forever.' 'Whoever or whencesoever you are,' returned the Arab, 'your dress and that of your servants show your rank to be high and your wealth to be great. Why should you, who can so easily procure your ransom, think yourself in danger of perpetual captivity? The purpose in my incursions is to increase my riches or, more properly, to gather tribute. The sons of Ishmael are the natural and hereditary lords of this part of the continent, which is usurped by late invaders and low-born tyrants, from whom we are compelled to take by the sword what is denied to justice. The violence of war admits no distinctions; the lance that is lifted at guilt and power will sometimes fall on innocence and gentleness.'

" 'How little,' said I, 'did I expect that yesterday it should have fallen upon me!'

" 'Misfortunes,' answered the Arab, 'should always be expected. If the eye of hostility could learn reverence or pity, excellence like yours had been exempt from injury. But the angels of affliction spread their toils alike for the virtuous and the wicked, for the mighty and the mean. Do not be disconsolate. I am not one of the lawless and cruel rovers of the desert; I know the rules of civil life; I will fix your ransom, give a passport to your messenger, and perform my stipulation with nice punctuality.'

"You will easily believe that I was pleased with his courtesy, and, finding that his predominant passion was desire of money, I began now to think my danger less, for I knew that no sum would be thought too great for the release of Pekuah. I told him that he should have no reason to charge me with ingratitude, if I was used with kindness, and that any ransom which could be expected for a maid of common rank would be paid, but that he must not persist to rate me as a princess. He said he would consider what he should demand, and then, smiling, bowed and retired.

"Soon after, the women came about me, each contending to be more officious than the other, and my maids themselves were served with reverence. We travelled onward by short journeys. On the fourth day, the chief told me that my ransom must be two hundred ounces of gold; which I not only promised him, but told him that I would add fifty more, if I and my maids were honorably treated.

"I never knew the power of gold before. From that time I was the leader of the troop. The march of every day was longer or shorter as I commanded, and the tents were pitched where I chose to rest. We now had camels and other conveniences for travel; my own women were always at my side; and I amused myself with observing the manners of the vagrant nations and with viewing remains of ancient edifices, with which these deserted countries appear to have been, in some distant age, lavishly embellished.

"The chief of the band was a man far from illiterate. He was able to travel by the stars or the compass, and had marked, in his erratic expeditions, such places as are most worthy the notice of a stranger. He observed to me that buildings are always best preserved in places little frequented and difficult of access; for, when once a country declines from its primitive splendor, the more inhabitants are left, the quicker ruin will be made. Walls supply stones more easily than quarries, and palaces and temples will be demolished to make stables of granite and cottages of porphyry.

The Adventures of Pekuah Continued

39 "WE wandered about in this manner for some weeks, whether, as our chief pretended, for my gratification, or, as I rather suspected, for some convenience of his own. I endeavored to appear contented, where sullenness and resentment would have been of no use, and that endeavor conduced much to the calmness of my mind; but my heart was always with Nekayah, and the troubles of the night much overbalanced the amusements of the day. My women, who threw all their cares upon their mistress, set their minds at ease from the time when they saw me treated with respect, and gave themselves up to the incidental alleviations of our fatigue without solicitude or sorrow. I was pleased with their pleasure, and animated with their confidence. My condition had lost much of its terror, since I found that the Arab ranged the country merely to get riches. Avarice is an uniform and tractable vice. Other intellectual distempers are different in different constitutions of mind; that which soothes the pride of

one will offend the pride of another, but to the favor of the covetous there is a ready way. Bring money, and nothing is denied.

"At last we came to the dwelling of our chief, a strong and spacious house built with stone in an island of the Nile, which lies, as I was told, under the tropic. 'Lady,' said the Arab, 'you shall rest after your journey a few weeks in this place, where you are to consider yourself as sovereign. My occupation is war. I have therefore chosen this obscure residence, from which I can issue unexpected and to which I can retire unpursued. You may now repose in security; here are few pleasures, but here is no danger.' He then led me into the inner apartments and, seating me on the richest couch, bowed to the ground. His women, who considered me as a rival, looked on me with malignity, but, being soon informed that I was a great lady detained only for my ransom, they began to vie with each other in obsequiousness and reverence.

"Being again comforted with new assurances of speedy liberty, I was for some days diverted from impatience by the novelty of the place. The turrets overlooked the country to a great distance, and afforded a view of many windings of the stream. In the day I wandered from one place to another, as the course of the sun varied the splendor of the prospect, and saw many things which I had never seen before. The crocodiles and river-horses are common in this unpeopled region, and I often looked upon them with terror, though I knew that they could not hurt me. For some time I expected to see mermaids and tritons, which, as

Imlac has told me, the European travellers have stationed in the Nile; but no such beings ever appeared, and the Arab, when I inquired after them, laughed at my credulity.

"At night the Arab always attended me to a tower set apart for celestial observations, where he endeavored to teach me the names and courses of the stars. I had no great inclination to this study, but an appearance of attention was necessary to please my instructor, who valued himself for his skill; and, in a little while, I found some employment requisite to beguile the tediousness of time, which was to be passed always amidst the same objects. I was weary of looking in the morning on things from which I had turned away weary in the evening; I therefore was at last willing to observe the stars rather than do nothing, but could not always compose my thoughts, and was very often thinking of Nekayah, when others imagined me contemplating the sky. Soon after, the Arab went upon another expedition, and then my only pleasure was to talk with my maids about the accident by which we were carried away and the happiness that we should all enjoy at the end of our captivity."

"There were women in your Arab's fortress," said the princess. "Why did you not make them your companions, enjoy their conversation, and partake their diversions? In a place where they found business or amusement, why should you alone sit corroded with idle melancholy? Or why could not you bear for a few months that condition to which they were condemned for life?"

"The diversions of the women," answered Pekuah, "were only childish play, by which the mind accustomed to stronger operations could not be kept busy. I could do all which they delighted in doing, by powers merely sensitive, while my intellectual faculties were flown to Cairo. They ran from room to room, as a bird hops from wire to wire in his cage. They danced for the sake of motion, as lambs frisk in a meadow. One sometimes pretended to be hurt that the rest might be alarmed, or hid herself that another might seek her. Part of their time passed in watching the progress of light bodies that floated on the river, and part in marking the various forms into which clouds broke in the sky.

"Their business was only needlework, in which I and my maids sometimes helped them; but you know that the mind will easily straggle from the fingers, nor will you suspect that captivity and absence from Nekayah could receive solace from silken flowers.

"Nor was much satisfaction to be hoped from their conversation, for of what could they be expected to talk? They had seen nothing, for they had lived from early youth in that narrow spot. Of what they had not seen, they could have no knowledge, for they could not read. They had no ideas but of the few things that were within their view, and had hardly names for anything but their clothes and their food. As I bore a superior character, I was often called to terminate their quarrels, which I decided as equitably as I could. If it could have amused me to hear the complaints of each against the rest, I might have been often detained by long stories, but the motives of their animosity were so small that I could not listen without intercepting the tale."

"How," said Rasselas, "can the Arab, whom you represented as a man of more than common accomplishments, take any pleasure in his seraglio, when it is filled only with women like these? Are they exquisitely beautiful?"

"They do not," said Pekuah, "want that unaffecting and ignoble beauty which may subsist without sprightliness or sublimity, without energy of thought or dignity of virtue. But to a man like the Arab such beauty was only a flower casually plucked and carelessly thrown away. Whatever pleasures he might find among them, they were not those of friendship or society. When they were playing about him, he looked on them with inattentive superiority; when they vied for his regard, he sometimes turned away disgusted. As they had no knowledge, their talk could take nothing from the tediousness of life; as they had no choice, their fondness, or appearance of fondness, excited in him neither pride nor gratitude; he was not exalted in his own esteem by the smiles of a woman who saw no other man, nor was much obliged by that regard of which he could never know the sincerity and which he might often perceive to be exerted, not so much to delight him, as to pain a rival. That which he gave and they received as love was only a careless distribution of superfluous time, such love as man can bestow upon that which he despises, such as has neither hope, nor fear, neither joy nor sorrow."

"You have reason, lady, to think yourself happy," said Imlac, "that you have been thus easily dismissed. How could a mind, hungry for knowledge, be willing, in an intellectual famine, to lose such a banquet as Pekuah's conversation?"

"I am inclined to believe," answered Pekuah, "that he was for some time in suspense; for, notwithstanding his promise, whenever I proposed to dispatch a messenger to Cairo, he found some excuse for delay. While I was detained in his house, he made many incursions into the neighboring countries; and, perhaps, he would have refused to discharge me, had his plunder been equal to his wishes. He returned always courteous, related his adventures, delighted to hear my observations, and endeavored to advance my acquaintance with the stars. When I importuned him to send away my letters, he soothed me with professions of honor and sincerity; and, when I could be no longer decently denied, put his troop again in motion and left me to govern in his absence. I was much afflicted by this studied procrastination, and was sometimes afraid that I should be forgotten, that you would leave Cairo, and I must end my days in an island of the Nile.

"I grew at last hopeless and dejected, and cared so little to entertain him that he for a while more frequently talked with my maids. That he should fall in love with them, or with me, might have been equally fatal, and I was not much pleased with the growing friendship. My anxiety was not long; for, as I recovered some degree of cheerfulness, he returned to me, and I could not forbear to despise my former uneasiness.

"He still delayed to send for my ransom and would, perhaps, never have determined, had not your agent found his way to him. The gold, which he would not fetch, he could not reject when it was offered. He hastened to prepare for our journey hither, like a man delivered from the pain of an intestine conflict. I took leave of my companions in the house, who dismissed me with cold indifference."

Nekayah, having heard her favorite's relation, rose and embraced her, and Rasselas gave her an hundred ounces of gold, which she presented to the Arab for the fifty that were promised.

The History of a Man of Learning

40 THEY returned to Cairo and were so well pleased at finding themselves together that none of them went much abroad. The prince began to love learning, and one day declared to Imlac that he intended to devote himself to science and pass the rest of his days in literary solitude.

"Before you make your final choice," answered Imlac, "you ought to examine its hazards and converse with some of those who are grown old in the company of themselves. I have just left the observatory of one of the most learned astronomers in the world, who has spent forty years in unwearied attention to the motions and appearances of the celestial bodies, and has drawn out his soul in endless calculations. He admits a few friends once a month to hear his deductions and enjoy his discoveries. I was introduced as a man of knowledge worthy of his notice. Men of various ideas and fluent conversation are commonly welcome to those whose thoughts have been long fixed upon a single point and who find the images of other things stealing away. I delighted him with my remarks; he smiled at the narrative of my travels, and was glad to forget the constellations and descend for a moment into the lower world.

"On the next day of vacation I renewed my visit, and was so fortunate as to please him again. He relaxed from that time the severity of his rule, and permitted me to enter at my own choice. I found him always busy and always glad to be relieved. As each knew much which the other was desirous of learning, we exchanged our notions with great delight. I perceived that I had every day more of his confidence, and always found new cause of admiration in the profundity of his mind. His comprehension is vast, his memory capacious and retentive, his discourse is methodical, and his expression clear.

"His integrity and benevolence are equal to his learning. His deepest researches and most favorite studies are willingly interrupted for any opportunity of doing good by his counsel or his riches. To his closest retreat, at his most busy moments, all are admitted that want his assistance. 'For though I exclude idleness and pleasure, I will never,' says he, 'bar my doors against charity. To man is permitted the contemplation of the skies, but the practice of virtue is commanded.' "

"Surely," said the princess, "this man is happy."

"I visited him," said Imlac, "with more and more frequency, and was every time more enamored of his conversation; he was sublime without haughtiness, courteous without formality, and communicative without ostentation. I was at first, great princess, of your opinion, thought him the happiest of mankind, and often congratulated him on the blessing that he enjoyed. He seemed to hear nothing with indifference but the praises of his condition, to which he always returned a general answer, and diverted the conversation to some other topic.

"Amidst this willingness to be pleased and labor to please, I had quickly reason to imagine that some painful sentiment pressed upon his mind. He often looked up earnestly towards the sun, and let his voice fall in the midst of his discourse. He would sometimes, when we were alone, gaze upon me in silence, with the air of a man who longed to speak what he was yet resolved to suppress. He would often send for me with vehement injunctions of haste, though when I came to him, he had nothing extraordinary to say, and, sometimes when I was leaving him, would call me back, pause a few moments, and then dismiss me.

The Astronomer Discovers the Cause of His Uneasiness

41 "AT last the time came when the secret burst his reserve. We were sitting together last night in the turret of his house, watching the emersion of a satellite of Jupiter. A sudden tempest clouded the sky and disappointed our observation. We sat a while silent in the dark, and then he addressed himself to me in these words: 'Imlac, I have long considered thy friendship as the greatest blessing of my life. Integrity without knowledge is weak and useless, and knowledge without integrity is dangerous and dreadful. I have found in thee all the qualities requisite for trust: benevolence, experience, and fortitude. I have long discharged an office which I must soon quit at the call of nature, and shall rejoice in the hour of imbecility and pain to devolve it upon thee.'

"I thought myself honored by this testimony, and protested that whatever could conduce to his appiness would add likewise to mine.

" 'Hear, Imlac, what thou wilt not without difficulty credit. I have possessed for five years the regulation of the weather and the distribution of the seasons. The sun has listened to my dictates and passed from tropic to tropic by my direction; the clouds, at my call, have poured their waters, and the Nile has overflowed at my command; I have restrained the rage of the dog-star, and mitigated the fervors of the Crab. The winds alone, of all the elemental powers, have hitherto refused my authority, and multitudes have perished by equinoctial tempests, which I found myself unable to prohibit or restrain. I have administered this great office with exact justice, and made to the different nations of the earth an impartial dividend of rain and sunshine. What must have been the misery of half the globe, if I had limited the clouds to particular regions or confined the sun to either side of the equator?'

The Opinion of the Astronomer Is Explained and Justified

42   "ı suppose he discovered in me, through the obscurity of the room, some tokens of amazement and doubt, for, after a short pause, he proceeded thus:

" 'Not to be easily credited will neither surprise nor offend me; for I am, probably, the first of human beings to whom this trust has been imparted. Nor do I know whether to deem this distinction a reward or punishment. Since I have possessed it, I have been far less happy than before, and nothing but the consciousness of good intention could have enabled me to support the weariness of unremitted vigilance.'

" 'How long, sir,' said I, 'has this great office been in your hands?'

" 'About ten years ago,' said he, 'my daily observations of the changes of the sky led me to consider whether, if I had the power of the seasons, I could confer greater plenty upon the inhabitants of the earth. This contemplation fastened on my mind, and I sat days and nights in imaginary dominion, pouring upon this country and that the showers of fertility, and seconding every fall of rain with a due proportion of sunshine. I had yet only the will to do good, and did not imagine that I should ever have the power.

" 'One day, as I was looking on the fields withering with heat, I felt in my mind a sudden wish that I could send rain on the southern mountains, and raise the Nile to an inundation. In the hurry of my imagination, I commanded rain to fall, and, by comparing the time of my command with that of the inundation, I found that the clouds had listened to my lips.'

" 'Might not some other cause,' said I, 'produce this concurrence? The Nile does not always rise on the same day.'

" 'Do not believe,' said he with impatience, 'that such objections could escape me. I reasoned long against my own conviction, and labored against truth with the utmost obstinacy. I sometimes suspected myself of madness, and should not have dared to impart this secret but to a man like you, capable of distinguishing the wonderful from the impossible and the incredible from the false.'

" 'Why, sir,' said I, 'do you call that incredible, which you know, or think you know, to be true?'

" 'Because,' said he, 'I cannot prove it by any external evidence, and I know too well the laws of demonstration to think that my conviction ought to influence another who cannot, like me, be conscious of its force. I therefore shall not

attempt to gain credit by disputation. It is sufficient that I feel this power, that I have long
possessed and every day exerted it. But the life
of man is short, the infirmities of age increase
upon me, and the time will soon come when the
regulator of the year must mingle with the dust.
The care of appointing a successor has long disturbed me; the night and the day have been spent
in comparisons of all characters which have come
to my knowledge, and I have yet found none so
worthy as thyself.'

The Astronomer Leaves Imlac His Directions

43   " 'HEAR, therefore, what I shall impart, with attention such as the welfare of a world requires. If the task of a king be considered as difficult, who has the care only of a few millions, to whom he cannot do much good or harm, what must be the anxiety of him on whom depends the action of the elements and the great gifts of light and heat! Hear me therefore with attention.

" 'I have diligently considered the position of the earth and sun, and formed innumerable schemes in which I changed their situation. I have sometimes turned aside the axis of the earth, and sometimes varied the ecliptic of the sun; but I have found it impossible to make a disposition by which the world may be advantaged. What one region gains, another loses, by an imaginable alteration, even without considering the distant parts of the solar system with which we are unacquainted. Do not, therefore, in thy administration of the year, indulge thy pride by innovation; do not please thyself with thinking that thou canst make thyself renowned to all future ages by disordering the seasons. The memory of mischief is no desirable fame. Much less will it become thee to let kindness or interest prevail. Never rob other countries of rain to pour it on thine own. For us the Nile is sufficient.'

"I promised that, when I possessed the power, I would use it with inflexible integrity, and he dismissed me, pressing my hand. 'My heart,' said he, 'will be now at rest, and my benevolence will no more destroy my quiet; I have found a man of wisdom and virtue, to whom I can cheerfully bequeath the inheritance of the sun.' "

The prince heard this narration with very serious regard; but the princess smiled, and Pekuah convulsed herself with laughter. "Ladies," said Imlac, "to mock the heaviest of human afflictions is neither charitable nor wise. Few can attain this man's knowledge, and few practice his virtues; but all may suffer his calamity. Of the uncertainties of our present state, the most dreadful and alarming is the uncertain continuance of reason."

The princess was recollected, and the favorite was abashed. Rasselas, more deeply affected, inquired of Imlac whether he thought such maladies of the mind frequent and how they were contracted.

The Dangerous Prevalence of Imagination

44 "DISORDERS of intellect," answered Imlac, "happen much more often than superficial observers will easily believe. Perhaps, if we speak with rigorous exactness, no human mind is in its right state. There is no man whose imagination does not sometimes predominate over his reason, who can regulate his attention wholly by his will and whose ideas will come and go at his command. No man will be found in whose mind airy notions do not sometimes tyrannize and force him to hope or fear beyond the limits of sober probability. All power of fancy over reason is a degree of insanity, but, while this power is such as we can control and repress, it is not visible to others, nor considered as any depravation of the mental faculties. It is not pronounced madness but when it becomes ungovernable and apparently influences speech or action.

"To indulge the power of fiction and send imagination out upon the wing is often the sport of those who delight too much in silent speculation. When we are alone, we are not always busy; the labor of excogitation is too violent to last long; the ardor of inquiry will sometimes give way to idleness or satiety. He who has nothing external that can divert him must find pleasure in his own thoughts, and must conceive himself what he is not, for who is pleased with what he is? He then expatiates in boundless futurity, and culls from all imaginable conditions that which for the present moment he should most desire, amuses his desires with impossible enjoyments, and confers upon his pride unattainable dominion. The mind dances from scene to scene, unites all pleasures in all combinations, and riots in delights which nature and fortune, with all their bounty, cannot bestow.

"In time some particular train of ideas fixes the attention; all other intellectual gratifications are rejected; the mind, in weariness or leisure, recurs constantly to the favorite conception, and feasts on the luscious falsehood whenever she is offended with the bitterness of truth. By degrees the reign of fancy is confirmed; she grows first imperious and, in time, despotic. Then fictions begin to operate as realities, false opinions fasten upon the mind, and life passes in dreams of rapture or of anguish.

"This, sir, is one of the dangers of solitude, which the hermit has confessed not always to promote goodness and the astronomer's misery has proved to be not always propitious to wisdom."

"I will no more," said the favorite, "imagine

myself the Queen of Abyssinia. I have often spent the hours which the princess gave to my own disposal in adjusting cermonies and regulating the court; I have repressed the pride of the powerful and granted the petitions of the poor; I have built new palaces in more happy situations, planted groves upon the tops of mountains, and have exulted in the beneficence of royalty till, when the princess entered, I had almost forgotten to bow down before her."

"And I," said the princess, "will not allow myself any more to play the shepherdess in my waking dreams. I have often soothed my thoughts with the quiet and innocence of pastoral employments, till I have in my chamber heard the winds whistle and the sheep bleat; sometimes freed the lamb entangled in the thicket, and sometimes with my crook encountered the wolf. I have a dress like that of the village maids, which I put on to help my imagination, and a pipe on which I play softly and suppose myself followed by my flocks."

"I will confess," said the prince, "an indulgence of fantastic delight more dangerous than yours. I have frequently endeavored to image the possibility of a perfect government, by which all wrong should be restrained, all vice reformed, and all the subjects preserved in tranquillity and innocence. This thought produced innumerable schemes of reformation and dictated many useful regulations and salutary edicts. This has been the sport and sometimes the labor of my solitude, and I start when I think with how little anguish I once supposed the death of my father and my brothers."

"Such," says Imlac, "are the effects of visionary schemes. When we first form them, we know them to be absurd, but familiarize them by degrees, and in time lose sight of their folly."

They Discourse with an Old Man

45 THE evening was now far past, and they rose to return home. As they walked along the bank of the Nile, delighted with the beams of the moon quivering on the water, they saw at a small distance an old man, whom the prince had often heard in the assembly of the sages. "Yonder," said he, "is one whose years have calmed his passions, but not clouded his reason. Let us close the disquisitions of the night by inquiring what are his sentiments of his own state, that we may know whether youth alone is to struggle with vexation and whether any better hope remains for the latter part of life."

Here the sage approached and saluted them. They invited him to join their walk and prattled a while, as acquaintances that had unexpectedly met one another. The old man was cheerful and talkative, and the way seemed short in his company. He was pleased to find himself not disregarded, accompanied them to their house, and, at the prince's request, entered with them. They placed him in the seat of honor, and set wine and conserves before him.

"Sir," said the princess, "an evening walk must give a man of learning, like you, pleasures which ignorance and youth can hardly conceive. You know the qualities and the causes of all that you behold, the laws by which the river flows, the periods in which the planets perform their revolutions. Everything must supply you with contemplation, and renew the consciousness of your own dignity."

"Lady," answered he, "let the gay and the vigorous expect pleasure in their excursions; it is enough that age can obtain ease. To me the world has lost its novelty. I look round, and see what I remember to have seen in happier days. I rest against a tree, and consider that in the same shade I once disputed upon the annual overflow of the Nile with a friend who is now silent in the grave. I cast my eyes upwards, fix them on the changing moon, and think with pain on the vicissitudes of life. I have ceased to take much delight in physical truth, for what have I to do with those things which I am soon to leave?"

"You may at least recreate yourself," said Imlac, "with the recollection of an honorable and useful life, and enjoy the praise which all agree to give you."

"Praise," said the sage with a sigh, "is to an old man an empty sound. I have neither mother to be delighted with the reputation of her son, nor wife to partake the honors of her husband. I have outlived my friends and my rivals. Nothing is now of much importance, for I cannot extend my interest beyond myself. Youth is delighted with applause, because it is considered as the earnest of some future good and because the prospect of life is far extended; but to me, who am now declining to decrepitude, there is little to be feared from the malevolence of men, and yet less to be hoped from their affection or esteem. Something they may yet take away, but they can give me nothing. Riches would now be useless, and high employment would be pain. My retrospect of life recalls to my view many opportunities of good neglected, much time squandered upon trifles, and more lost in idleness and vacancy. I leave many great designs unattempted and many great attempts unfinished. My mind is burdened with no heavy crime, and therefore I compose myself to tranquillity; endeavor to abstract my thoughts from hopes and cares which, though reason knows them to be vain, still try to keep their old possession of the heart; expect, with serene humility, that hour which nature cannot long delay; and hope to possess, in a better state, that happiness which here I could not find and that virtue which here I have not attained."

He rose and went away, leaving his audience not much elated with the hope of long life. The prince consoled himself with remarking that it was not reasonable to be disappointed by this account, for age had never been considered as the season of felicity; and, if it was possible to be easy in decline and weakness, it was likely that the days of vigor and alacrity might be happy, that the noon of life might be bright, if the evening could be calm.

The princess suspected that age was querulous and malignant, and delighted to repress the expectations of those who had newly entered the world. She had seen the possessors of estates look with envy on their heirs, and known many who enjoyed pleasure no longer than they can confine it to themselves.

Pekuah conjectured that the man was older than he appeared, and was willing to impute his complaints to delirious dejection, or else suppose that he had been unfortunate and was therefore discontented. "For nothing," said she, "is more common than to call our own condition the condition of life."

Imlac, who had no desire to see them depressed, smiled at the comforts which they could so readily procure to themselves, and remembered that at the same age he was equally confident of unmingled prosperity and equally fertile of consolatory expedients. He forbore to force upon them unwelcome knowledge, which time itself would too soon impress. The princess and her lady retired; the madness of the astronomer hung upon their minds, and they desired Imlac to enter upon his office, and delay next morning the rising of the sun.

The Princess and Pekuah Visit the Astronomer

46   THE princess and Pekuah, having talked in private of Imlac's astronomer, thought his character at once so amiable and so strange that they could not be satisfied without nearer knowledge, and Imlac was requested to find the means of bringing them together.

This was somewhat difficult. The philosopher had never received any visits from women, though he lived in a city that had in it many Europeans, who followed the manners of their own countries, and many from other parts of the world, that lived there with European liberty. The ladies would not be refused, and several schemes were proposed for the accomplishment of their design. It was proposed to introduce them as strangers in distress, to whom the sage was always accessible; but, after some deliberation, it appeared that by this artifice no acquaintance could be formed, for their conversation would be short, and they could not decently importune him often. "This," said Rasselas, "is true, but I have yet a stronger objection against the misrepresentation of your state. I have always considered it as treason against the great republic of human nature to make any man's virtues the means of deceiving him, whether on great or little occasions. All imposture weakens confidence and chills benevolence. When the sage finds that you are not what you seemed, he will feel the resentment natural to a man who, conscious of great abilities, discovers that he has been tricked by understandings meaner than his own; and, perhaps, the distrust, which he can never afterwards wholly lay aside, may stop the voice of counsel and close the hand of charity; and where will you find the power of restoring his benefactions to mankind, or his peace to himself?"

To this no reply was attempted, and Imlac began to hope that their curiosity would subside; but, next day, Pekuah told him, she had now found an honest pretense for a visit to the astronomer, for she would solicit permission to continue under him the studies in which she had been initiated by the Arab, and the princess might go with her either as a fellow student or because a woman could not decently come alone. "I am afraid," said Imlac, "that he will be soon weary of your company; men advanced far in knowledge do not love to repeat the elements of their art, and I am not certain that even of the elements, as he will deliver them, connected with inferences and mingled with reflections, you are a very capable auditress." "That," said Pekuah, "must be my care; I ask of you only to take me thither. My knowledge is, perhaps, more than you imagine it, and, by concurring always with his opinions, I shall make him think it greater than it is."

The astronomer, in pursuance of this resolution, was told that a foreign lady, travelling in search of knowledge, had heard of his reputation and was desirous to become his scholar. The uncommonness of the proposal raised at once his surprise and curiosity; and when, after a short deliberation, he consented to admit her, he could not stay without impatience till the next day.

The ladies dressed themselves magnificently, and were attended by Imlac to the astronomer, who was pleased to see himself approached with respect by persons of so splendid an appearance. In the exchange of the first civilities, he was timorous and bashful; but, when the talk became regular, he recollected his powers and justified the character which Imlac had given. Inquiring of Pekuah what could have turned her inclination towards astronomy, he received from her a history of her adventure at the Pyramid and of the time passed in the Arab's island. She told her tale with ease and elegance, and her conversation took possession of his heart. The discourse was then turned to astronomy. Pekuah displayed what she knew; he looked upon her as a prodigy of genius, and entreated her not to desist from a study which she had so happily begun.

They came again and again, and were every time more welcome than before. The sage endeavored to amuse them, that they might prolong their visits, for he found his thoughts grow brighter in their company; the clouds of solicitude vanished by degrees, as he forced himself to entertain them, and he grieved when he was left at their departure to his old employment of regulating the seasons.

The princess and her favorite had now watched his lips for several months, and could not catch a single word from which they could judge whether he continued, or not, in the opinion of his preternatural commission. They often contrived to bring him to an open declaration, but he easily eluded all their attacks and, on which side soever they pressed him, escaped from them to some other topic.

As their familiarity increased, they invited him often to the house of Imlac, where they distinguished him by extraordinary respect. He began gradually to delight in sublunary pleasures. He came early and departed late; labored to recommend himself by assiduity and compliance; excited their curiosity after new arts, that they might still want his assistance; and, when they made any excursion of pleasure or inquiry, entreated to attend them.

By long experience of his integrity and wisdom, the prince and his sister were convinced that he might be trusted without danger, and, lest he should draw any false hopes from the civilities which he received, discovered to him their condition, with the motives of their journey, and required his opinion on the choice of life.

"Of the various conditions which the world spreads before you, which you shall prefer," said the sage, "I am not able to instruct you. I can only tell that I have chosen wrong. I have passed my time in study without experience; in the attainment of sciences which can, for the most part, be remotely useful to mankind. I have purchased knowledge at the expense of all the common comforts of life; I have missed the endearing elegance of female friendship and the happy commerce of domestic tenderness. If I have obtained any prerogatives above other students, they have been accompanied with fear, disquiet, and scrupulosity; but even of these prerogatives, whatever they were, I have, since my thoughts have been diversified by more intercourse with the world, begun to question the reality. When I have been for a few days lost in pleasing dissipation, I am always tempted to think that my inquiries have ended in error and that I have suffered much and suffered it in vain."

Imlac was delighted to find that the sage's understanding was breaking through its mists, and resolved to detain him from the planets, till he should forget his task of ruling them and reason should recover its original influence.

From this time the astronomer was received into familiar friendship, and partook of all their projects and pleasures; his respect kept him attentive, and the activity of Rasselas did not leave much time unengaged. Something was always to be done; the day was spent in making observations which furnished talk for the evening, and the evening was closed with a scheme for the morrow.

The sage confessed to Imlac that, since he had mingled in the gay tumults of life and divided his hours by a succession of amusements, he found the conviction of his authority over the skies fade gradually from his mind, and began to trust less to an opinion which he never could prove to others and which he now found subject to variation, from causes in which reason had no part. "If I am accidentally left alone for a few hours," said he, "my inveterate persuasion rushes upon my soul, and my thoughts are chained down by irresistible violence; but they are soon disentangled by the prince's conversation, and instantaneously released at the entrance of Pekuah. I am like a man habitually afraid of spectres, who is set at ease by a lamp and wonders at the dread which harassed him in the dark; yet, if his lamp be extinguished, feels again the terrors which he knows that when it is light he shall feel no more. But I am sometimes afraid lest I indulge my quiet by criminal negligence and voluntarily forget the great charge with which I am entrusted. If I favor myself in a known error or am determined by my own ease in a doubtful question of this importance, how dreadful is my crime!"

"No disease of the imagination," answered Imlac, "is so difficult of cure as that which is complicated with the dread of guilt; fancy and conscience then act interchangeably upon us and so often shift their places that the illusions of one are not distinguished from the dictates of the other. If fancy presents images not moral or religious, the mind drives them away when they give it pain; but, when melancholic notions take the form of duty, they lay hold on the faculties without opposition, because we are afraid to exclude or banish them. For this reason the superstitious are often melancholy, and the melancholy almost always superstitious.

"But do not let the suggestions of timidity overpower your better reason; the danger of neglect can be but as the probability of the obligation, which, when you consider it with freedom, you find very little, and that little growing every day less. Open your heart to the influence of the light which from time to time breaks in upon you; when scruples importune you, which you in your lucid moments know to be vain, do not stand to parley, but fly to business, or to Pekuah; and keep this thought always prevalent, that you are only one atom of the mass of humanity and have neither such virtue nor vice as that you should be singled out for supernatural favors or afflictions."

The Prince Enters and
Brings a New Topic

47 "ALL this," said the astronomer, "I have often thought, but my reason has been so long subjugated by an uncontrollable and overwhelming idea that it durst not confide in its own decisions. I now see how fatally I betrayed my quiet by suffering chimeras to prey upon me in secret; but melancholy shrinks from communication, and I never found a man before to whom I could impart my troubles, though I had been certain of relief. I rejoice to find my own sentiments confirmed by yours, who are not easily deceived and can have no motive or purpose to deceive. I hope that time and variety will dissipate the gloom that has so long surrounded me, and the latter part of my days will be spent in peace."

"Your learning and virtue," said Imlac, "may justly give you hopes."

Rasselas then entered with the princess and Pekuah, and inquired whether they had contrived any new diversion for the next day. "Such," said Nekayah, "is the state of life, that none are happy but by the anticipation of change; the change itself is nothing. When we have made it, the next wish is to change again. The world is not yet exhausted; let me see something tomorrow which I never saw before."

"Variety," said Rasselas, "is so necessary to content that even the happy valley disgusted me by the recurrence of its luxuries; yet I could not forbear to reproach myself with impatience when I saw the monks of St. Anthony support, without complaint, a life not of uniform delight, but uniform hardship."

"Those men," answered Imlac, "are less wretched in their silent convent than the Abyssinian princes in their prison of pleasure. Whatever is done by the monks is incited by an adequate and reasonable motive. Their labor supplies them with necessaries; it therefore cannot be omitted, and is certainly rewarded. Their devotion prepares them for another state, and reminds them of its approach while it fits them for it. Their time is regularly distributed. One duty succeeds another, so that they are not left open to the distraction of unguided choice nor left in the shades of listless inactivity. There is a certain task to be performed at an appropriated hour, and their toils are cheerful because they consider them as acts of piety by which they are always advancing towards endless felicity."

"Do you think," said Nekayah, "that the monastic rule is a more holy and less imperfect state than any other? May not he equally hope for future happiness who converses openly with mankind, who succors the distressed by his charity, instructs the ignorant by his learning, and contributes by his industry to the general system of life, even though he should omit some of the mortifications which are practiced in the cloister and allow himself such harmless delights as his condition may place within his reach?"

"This," said Imlac, "is a question which has long divided the wise and perplexed the good. I am afraid to decide on either part. He that lives well in the world is better than he that lives well in a monastery. But, perhaps, everyone is not able to stem the temptations of public life, and, if he cannot conquer, he may properly retreat. Some have little power to do good, and have likewise little strength to resist evil. Many are weary of their conflicts with adversity, and are willing to eject those passions which have long busied them in vain. And many are dismissed by age and diseases from the more laborious duties of society. In monasteries, the weak and timorous may be happily sheltered, the weary may repose, and the penitent may meditate. Those retreats of prayer and comtemplation have something so congenial to the mind of man that, perhaps, there is scarcely one that does not purpose to close his life in pious abstraction, with a few associates serious as himself."

"Such," said Pekuah, "has often been my wish, and I have heard the princess declare that she would not willingly die in a crowd."

"The liberty of using harmless pleasures," proceeded Imlac, "will not be disputed, but it is still to be examined what pleasures are harmless. The evil of any pleasure that Nekayah can image is not in the act itself, but in its consequences. Pleasure in itself harmless may become mischievous by endearing to us a state which we know to be transient and probatory, and withdrawing our thoughts from that of which every hour brings us nearer to the beginning and of which no length of time will bring us to the end. Mortification is not virtuous in itself, nor has any other use, but that it disengages us from the allurements of sense. In the state of future perfection, to which we all aspire, there will be pleasure without danger and security without restraint."

The princess was silent, and Rasselas, turning to the astronomer, asked him whether he could not delay her retreat, by showing her something which she had not seen before.

"Your curiosity," said the sage, "has been so general, and your pursuit of knowledge so vigorous, that novelties are not now very easily to be found; but what you can no longer procure from the living may be given by the dead. Among the wonders of this country are the Catacombs or the ancient repositories in which the bodies of the earliest generations were lodged and where, by the virtue of the gums which embalmed them, they yet remain without corruption."

"I know not," said Rasselas, "what pleasure the sight of the Catacombs can afford; but, since nothing else is offered, I am resolved to view them, and shall place this with many other things which I have done because I would do something."

They hired a guard of horsemen, and the next day visited the Catacombs. When they were about to descend into the sepulchral caves, "Pekuah," said the princess, "we are now again invading the habitations of the dead; I know that you will stay behind; let me find you safe when I return." "No, I will not be left," answered Pekuah. "I will go down between you and the prince."

They then all descended, and roved with wonder through the labyrinth of subterraneous passages, where the bodies were laid in rows on either side.

Imlac Discourses on the Nature of the Soul

48 "WHAT reason," said the prince, "can be given why the Egyptians should thus expensively preserve those carcasses, which some nations consume with fire, others lay to mingle with the earth, and all agree to remove from their sight as soon as decent rites can be performed?"

"The original of ancient customs," said Imlac, "is commonly unknown, for the practice often continues when the cause has ceased, and concerning superstitious ceremonies it is vain to conjecture, for what reason did not dictate, reason cannot explain. I have long believed that the practice of embalming arose only from tenderness to the remains of relations or friends; and to this opinion I am more inclined, because it seems impossible that this care should have been general. Had all the dead been embalmed, their repositories must in time have been more spacious than the dwellings of the living. I suppose only the rich or honorable were secured from corruption, and the rest left to the course of nature.

"But it is commonly supposed that the Egyptians believed the soul to live as long as the body continued undissolved, and therefore tried this method of eluding death."

"Could the wise Egyptians," said Nekayah, "think so grossly of the soul? If the soul could once survive its separation, what could it afterwards receive or suffer from the body?"

"The Egyptians would doubtless think erroneously," said the astronomer, "in the darkness of heathenism and the first dawn of philosophy. The nature of the soul is still disputed, amidst all our opportunities of clearer knowledge. Some yet say that it may be material, who, nevertheless, believe it to be immortal."

"Some," answered Imlac, "have indeed said that the soul is material, but I can scarcely believe that any man has thought it, who knew how to think; for all the conclusions of reason enforce the immateriality of mind, and all the notices of sense and investigations of science concur to prove the unconsciousness of matter.

"It was never supposed that cogitation is inherent in matter or that every particle is a thinking being. Yet, if any part of matter be devoid of thought, what part can we suppose to think? Matter can differ from matter only in form, density, bulk, motion, and direction of motion. To which of these, however varied or combined, can consciousness be annexed? To be round or square, to be solid or fluid, to be great or little, to be moved slowly or swiftly one way or another, are modes of material existence, all equally alien from the nature of cogitation. If matter be once without thought, it can only be made to think by some new modification; but all the modifications which it can admit are equally unconnected with cogitative powers."

"But the materialists," said the astronomer, "urge that matter may have qualities with which we are unacquainted."

"He who will determine," returned Imlac, "against that which he knows, because there may be something which he knows not, — he that can set hypothetical possibility against acknowledged certainty — is not to be admitted among reasonable beings. All that we know of matter is that matter is inert, senseless, and lifeless; and, if this conviction cannot be opposed but by referring us to something that we know not, we have all the evidence that human intellect can admit. If that which is known may be overruled by that which is unknown, no being, not omniscient, can arrive at certainty."

"Yet let us not," said the astronomer, "too arrogantly limit the Creator's power."

"It is no limitation of omnipotence," replied the poet, "to suppose that one thing is not consistent with another, that the same proposition cannot be at once true and false, that the same number cannot be even and odd, that cogitation cannot be conferred on that which is created incapable of cogitation."

"I know not," said Nekayah, "any great use of

this question. Does that immateriality, which, in my opinion, you have sufficiently proved, necessarily include eternal duration?"

"Of immateriality," said Imlac, "our ideas are negative, and therefore obscure. Immateriality seems to imply a natural power of perpetual duration as a consequence of exemption from all causes of decay; whatever perishes is destroyed by the solution of its contexture and separation of its parts; nor can we conceive how that which has no parts, and therefore admits no solution, can be naturally corrupted or impaired."

"I know not," said Rasselas, "how to conceive anything without extension; what is extended must have parts, and you allow that whatever has parts may be destroyed."

"Consider your own conceptions," replied Imlac, "and the difficulty will be less. You will find substance without extension. An ideal form is no less real than material bulk; yet an ideal form has no extension. It is no less certain, when you think on a pyramid, that your mind possesses the idea of a pyramid than that the pyramid itself is standing. What space does the idea of a pyramid occupy more than the idea of a grain of corn? Or how can either idea suffer laceration? As is the effect, such is the cause; as thought is, such is the power that thinks, a power impassive and indiscerptible."

"But the Being," said Nekayah, "whom I fear to name, the Being which made the soul, can destroy it."

"He surely can destroy it," answered Imlac, "since, however unperishable, it receives from a superior nature its power of duration. That it will not perish by any inherent cause of decay, or principle of corruption, may be shown by philosophy; but philosophy can tell no more. That it will not be annihilated by him that made it, we must humbly learn from higher authority."

The whole assembly stood a while silent and collected. "Let us return," said Rasselas, "from this scene of mortality. How gloomy would be these mansions of the dead to him who did not know that he should never die, that what now acts shall continue its agency, and what now thinks shall think on forever. Those that lie here stretched before us, the wise and the powerful of ancient times, warn us to remember the shortness of our present state. They were, perhaps, snatched away while they were busy, like us, in the choice of life."

"To me," said the princess, "the choice of life is become less important; I hope hereafter to think only on the choice of eternity."

They then hastened out of the caverns, and under the protection of their guard returned to Cairo.

The Conclusion,
in Which Nothing Is Concluded

49 IT was now the time of the inundation of the Nile. A few days after their visit to the Catacombs, the river began to rise.

They were confined to their house. The whole region, being under water, gave them no invitation to any excursions, and, being well supplied with materials for talk, they diverted themselves with comparisons of the different forms of life which they had observed and with various schemes of happiness which each of them had formed.

Pekuah was never so much charmed with any place as the convent of St. Anthony, where the Arab restored her to the princess, and wished only to fill it with pious maidens and to be made prioress of the order; she was weary of expectation and disgust, and would gladly be fixed in some unvariable state.

The princess thought that of all sublunary things knowledge was the best. She desired first to learn all sciences, and then proposed to found a college of learned women, in which she would preside, that, by conversing with the old and educating the young, she might divide her time between the acquisition and communication of wisdom, and raise up for the next age models of prudence and patterns of piety.

The prince desired a little kingdom, in which he might administer justice in his own person and see all the parts of government with his own eyes; but he could never fix the limits of his dominion and was always adding to the number of his subjects.

Imlac and the astronomer were contented to be driven along the stream of life, without directing their course to any particular port.

Of these wishes that they had formed, they well knew that none could be obtained. They deliberated a while what was to be done, and resolved, when the inundation should cease, to return to Abyssinia.

The End

SELECTED BIBLIOGRAPHY

Baker, Ernest A., "The Oriental Story from *Rasselas* to *Vathek*," *The History of the English Novel*, V, pp. 55-76. London, H. F. and G. Witherby, 1934.

Belloc, Hilaire, "On *Rasselas*," *Stories, Essays, and Poems* (Everyman Library), pp. 358-364. London, J. M. Dent & Sons, 1938.

Chesterton, G. K., "Introduction" to *Rasselas*. London, J. M. Dent & Sons, 1926.

Conant, Martha P., *The Oriental Tale in England in the Eighteenth Century*. New York, Columbia University Press, 1908.

Elledge, Scott, "The Background and Development in English Criticism of the Theories of Generality and Particularity," *PMLA*, LXII (March, 1947), pp. 147-182.

Emerson, Oliver F., "Introduction" to *Rasselas*. New York, Henry Holt & Co., 1895.

Hill, George Birkbeck, "Introduction" to *Rasselas*. Oxford, Clarendon Press, 1887.

Howells, William Dean, "Editor's Easy Chair," *Harpers*, CXXXI (July, 1915), pp. 310-313.

Jenkins, Harold D., "Some Aspects of the Background of *Rasselas*," *Studies in English in Honor of R. D. O'Leary and S. L. Whitcomb*, University of Kansas, 1940, pp. 8-14.

Joost, Nicholas, "The Whispers of Fancy, or the Meaning of *Rasselas*," *Modern Age*, I (Fall, 1957), pp. 166-173.

Kenney, William, "Johnson's *Rasselas* after Two Centuries," *Boston University Studies in English*, III (Summer, 1957), pp. 83-96.

Kolb, Gwin J., "The Structure of *Rasselas*," *PMLA*, LXVI (September, 1951), pp. 609-717.

Link, Frederick M., "*Rasselas* and the Quest for Happiness," *Boston University Studies in English*, III (Summer, 1957), pp. 121-123.

Powell, Lawrence F., "Rasselas," London *Times Literary Supplement*, February 22, 1923, p. 124.

Raleigh, Walter Alexander, "Rasselas," *The English Novel*, pp. 203-206. London, John Murray, 1894.

Scott, Sir Walter, "Johnson," *Lives of the Novelists*, pp. 155-162 (World's Classics edition). London, Oxford University Press, 1906.

Sewall, Richard B., "Rousseau's Second Discourse in England from 1755 to 1762," *Philological Quarterly*, XVII (April, 1938), pp. 105-111.

Tillotson, Geoffrey, "*Rasselas* and the *Persian Tales*," London *Times Literary Supplement*, August 29, 1935, p. 534.

Wahba, Magdi (ed.), *Bicentenary Essays on Rasselas*, Supplement to *Cairo Studies in English*. Cairo, U.A.R., S. O. P.-Press, 1959.

Warner, Oliver, "*Rasselas*: The Testament of a Romantic," *Bookman*, LXXXII (June, 1932), pp. 147-148.

Wimsatt, William K., Jr., "The Structure of the 'Concrete Universal' in Literature," *PMLA*, LXII (March, 1947), pp. 262-280.